D1176659

Purchased from
Multnomah County Library
Title Wave Used Bookstore
216 NE Knott St, Portland, OR
503-988-5021

11v11:

An Oral History of the Two Greatest High School Soccer Teams That Never Actually Existed

by

C.I. DeMann

This book is a work of fiction. Names, characters, places, and incidents are the product of the author's imagination or are used fictitiously. Any resemblance to actual events, locales, or persons, living or dead, is coincidental.

Copyright 2017 by C.I. DeMann

All rights reserved. This book may not be reproduced in whole or in part by any process without the express written permission of the copyright holder, except for the use of brief quotations in a book review.

11v11

West Sycamore High School
Starting XI

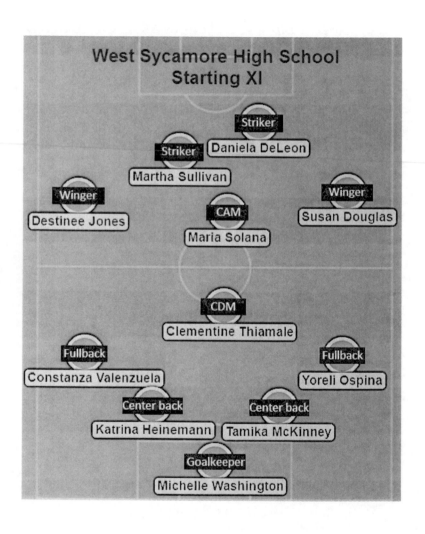

Striker
Daniela DeLeon

Striker
Martha Sullivan

Winger
Destinee Jones

CAM
Maria Solana

Winger
Susan Douglas

CDM
Clementine Thiamale

Fullback
Constanza Valenzuela

Fullback
Yoreli Ospina

Center back
Katrina Heinemann

Center back
Tamika McKinney

Goalkeeper
Michelle Washington

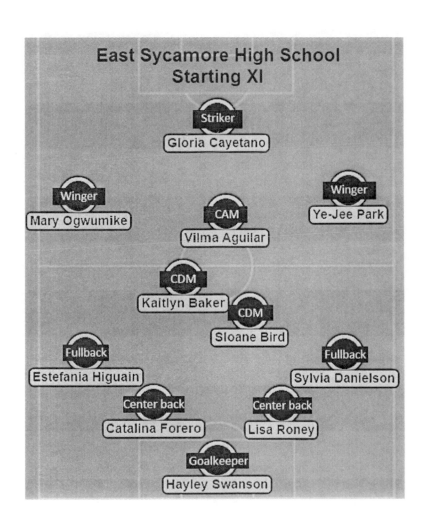

East Sycamore High School
Starting XI

Striker
Gloria Cayetano

Winger
Mary Ogwumike

CAM
Vilma Aguilar

Winger
Ye-Jee Park

CDM
Kaitlyn Baker

CDM
Sloane Bird

Fullback
Estefania Higuain

Fullback
Sylvia Danielson

Center back
Catalina Forero

Center back
Lisa Roney

Goalkeeper
Hayley Swanson

Though the United States is often considered a second-rate soccer nation, by raw numbers it's actually the #1 country in the world for participation at the youth level. This is especially true among girls. In the most recent FIFA global survey of registered youth players, 1.6 million girls were registered with the U.S. Soccer Federation, which was more than all other countries combined.

With so many American girls spending their formative years on a soccer pitch, it's no surprise that the U.S. Women's National Team has become a world power. And since they'd come into the most recent Women's World Cup in Argentina as the heavy favorite, the U.S. team's eventual 3-1 victory over Sweden in the championship game was not the story everyone was talking about.

The media on hand were much more fascinated to

discover that, ten years ago, five players in the tournament – from three different nations – had played high school soccer in the same American town.

Attending East Sycamore and West Sycamore High Schools, the five future internationals and their teammates – some future professionals themselves – rode dusty yellow school buses across town, playing each other multiple times, all while still teenagers. It's a concentration of talent that seems almost impossible and yet, ten years ago, it happened.

This is an oral history of that remarkable season, telling the story through the words of those who lived it. I've interviewed as many key participants as possible, some of them famous to millions, others known only to family and friends. Most were interviewed in person, a few over the phone, and everyone is listed with their position or job title from that year.

West Sycamore High School

Destinee Jones, left winger: That was my senior year, so I was thinking I was all big and bad. You know how it is when you're that age. You're 18, a senior, thinking you're ten feet tall and bulletproof. So I was definitely looking forward to the year. To being top dog. I was like, *Oh, man, life's gonna be so easy. I'll be showing up late, leaving early. Probably walk into class drinking a pumpkin spice latte. [laughs]* I guess that's what I thought it meant to be an adult. Walking around all day with a pumpkin spice latte.

But, soccer-wise, I wasn't expecting anything special that year. No one was. You gotta realize, back then, West Sycamore was a football school. My brothers all played football. Zak was the starting running back. He was the star in the family, not me. Nobody cared about

3

soccer, much less girls soccer. We were nobody. I'd been on the team three years, and I think we'd gone 7-7 every year. Maybe eight wins, tops. So, you know, going into that senior year, I figured it would be about the same.

I knew we were gonna have a new coach. Some lady. Nykesha Nolan. But what would that mean? Would everything change? Would nothing change? Somewhere in the middle? We didn't know.

All I knew was I wanted my pumpkin spice lattes. *[laughs]*

Susan Douglas, right winger: I didn't really have expectations. Back then, soccer wasn't about winning games or winning championships. Those things were cool, I guess, but for me, soccer was an escape. A way to escape my real life.

See, that year – I guess it was my junior year – that was, honest to God, one of the toughest years of my life. Maybe the toughest ever.

I know, right? Probably everyone else you interview, they're gonna say how amazing the year was, best year ever, that sort of thing, but for me, life kind of sucked back then. That year especially.

So, winning or losing? Good team or bad? I wasn't thinking about that. I just wanted to play soccer. Escape my crappy life for awhile.

Martha Sullivan, forward: That was my senior year, so there was all the usual senior stuff. You know, kings of the school, graduation coming up, all that.

I remember being pretty stressed about college. I didn't think I'd be able to go. My family, we weren't dirt poor or anything, but we definitely weren't rich. Not rich enough to pay for college.

Plus, my grades were only okay. My GPA was probably, like, 2.9, 3.0. Something like that. Not good enough to get an academic scholarship.

And I wasn't good enough to get an athletic scholarship, either. I mean, I'd scored two goals the year before. Schools don't come banging down your door if you've got stats like that, you know?

So I was like, *Dang, maybe I could join the Army or something. Get them to pay for college.* I didn't *want* to join the Army, but if I had to, maybe I would.

So that's what I was thinking about that year. Expectations for the team? Eight wins. Nine, maybe. Did I expect things to improve the way they did? No way. Not in my wildest dreams.

Clementine Thiamale, central defensive midfielder: That was my second year on the team. My second year in America. We'd come from Cote d'Ivoire.

My first year had been very hard. I had a tiny bit of English, but not a lot. Mostly French. And it's tough to feel comfortable when you're like that. You can be friendly to people and you can make friends with them, but there's only so deep you can go. You want to talk to them about everything, just like good friends do, but you can't. You don't know the words.

My best friend on the team was the goalkeeper Michelle Washington, because she spoke a little French. Only a little, though. I'd talk to her with my very simple English and she'd talk to me with her very simple French, and I know we both wanted to go deeper, but we couldn't. That's frustrating. It makes you feel like you'll never fit in.

But my second year, that was better. I started to feel like I belonged. My English was getting better. Michelle and I, we could talk a little more. Other girls, too. I was making friends, doing American things, meeting boys.

All of that would probably have been enough for me that year. If the soccer team had been only so-so, same as always, that would have been fine. I had plenty of other things going on, I just wanted the soccer to be fun.

But then we got a new coach. And Maria Solana came to town. Everything changed.

Nykesha Nolan, head coach: What did I expect? Are you kidding? I expected *everything*. *[laughs]* Win every game, state champions, conquer the world. Remember, I was 22 years old that year. Just outta college. Ink's not even dry on my diploma. So of course I was cocky. Thought I was God's gift to teaching. God's gift to coaching. *[laughs]*

I coached three sports that year. That's in addition to teaching P.E and Health. Crazy, right? The school told me to slow down, said it was too much on my plate, but I wasn't listening. I was like, *I just got done with a double major in college. I was a four-year starter in basketball* and *softball. You think I can't handle a busy schedule? [laughs]* It's funny, looking back on it. I didn't have a clue.

So, the soccer team... The truth is, my expectations weren't super high. Seven or eight wins? That was your typical girls soccer team back then. 7-7, 8-6, that sort of thing. I guess I thought we'd be a little better – maybe get to nine wins – just because I was so full of myself. But did I think we'd have the season we did? No way. That was Maria Solana, plain and simple.

Maria Solana, central attacking midfielder: Yes, I remember that year very well. Very well. I hope I can tell the story. My English, it's not as good these days. I don't get to speak it as much, you know. So maybe it is a little slow. What is the word? Rusty? Yes. My English is rusty.

So, that year... that was my first year in the United States. My family, we were from a tiny little town in Colombia. Very small. And that summer, we had moved to America. Very exciting, yes, but also very scary. I had no English then. None of my family did.

And that makes things very hard. Moving to a new country is always hard, but if you don't speak the language? So much worse. But my father, he said, "We are here to be Americans." So, very fast, we were taking lessons. A woman in our neighborhood, an old woman, she taught English at the church. Free lessons. So we were there, right from the beginning, me and my sisters, my mother and father. We really wanted to become Americans.

It is funny, isn't it? I worked so hard to become an American, and now I don't even live there anymore. But it was worth it. I learned a second language. I made friends.

The team, they were very good friends to me. Like a second family, you know, and that is a really good thing to have when you come to a new place. People who like you, who want to help you.

When I first came, I knew I wanted to play football, but did not know if the school would have a team. Because I had heard that football was not so big in the United States. Soccer, I mean. I had heard that *soccer* was not so big in the United States. And so when I got to school, I asked some of the girls if there was a team. The Latina girls. They said there was, but that it was not very good. I didn't mind. I just wanted to play, even if we were not good. I wanted to be part of something. When you are new to a place, you need that. Something to belong to.

For anyone who comes to America, I think that first

year is very hard. The language, the culture, the little differences. You feel like an outsider. And there are always some people who try to make you feel even worse. Like you're a bad person for coming to their country.

But with the soccer team, I felt like I belonged. A lot of immigrants, they do not have that, but I did. I had that team and that coach and all those girls. I will never forget them.

Nykesha Nolan, head coach: It's funny, looking back. Coaching the soccer team was kind of a last-minute thing. I'd just been hired, first-year teacher, and I wanted to coach. Basketball and softball, those would be easy. I played those sports, right? Easy. But those didn't start until winter and spring. What would I coach in the fall?

Oh, the soccer team needs a coach? Okay, yeah, I can do that. I don't know soccer, but whatever, I can learn. I can read books, I can watch video, I can talk to people.

That's kind of how it started. Just this last-minute thing. I certainly didn't think it would turn into this huge, gigantic success. I didn't think writers would be coming to me ten years later to talk about it.

And yet, here you are.

East Sycamore High School

Carlos Orostieta, head coach: Oh, what a year, what a year. My last year before retirement, you know, and what a way to go out! Such a group of girls, I loved them all. Though I guess I say that about all my girls. I coached 40 years, did you know that? 40 years! So many girls came through, I can't remember them all, but that last year, oh, yes, I remember them. Of course, some of them are still playing. Did you see the World Cup this last time? Four of my girls played. Four! Three from that last team. Not all starters, of course, but still, four players, that's quite an accomplishment, don't you think? Ah, yes, I was a lucky man, a very lucky man.

My expectations that season were high, very high. We'd done well the year before, made it all the way to the championship, so I knew we'd be good again. The defense, in particular. My goodness, what a defense we had that year! I never coached a defense so good. How many shutouts did we have? Eight? Nine? Ten? Someone told me we would've set a record if not for those last few games.

The offense, it was not as good. That was a frustration. We could never find a consistent goal scorer. A goal or two from this girl, a goal or two from that girl. There was never anyone on that team you could really count on to give you a goal when you needed it. Very frustrating. But the defense? Oh, the defense! Who needed goals with a defense like that? Best defense I ever coached. I mean that. 40 years, eight state titles, and that was the best defense I ever coached.

Catalina Forero, center back: Yeah, we were pretty loaded that year, weren't we? And experienced, too. Lot of seniors. I was a senior. Hayley Swanson was a senior. I figured one of us would be captain. Probably me. But, you know how things went with that. Oh, you don't? Well, good lord, what a mess. *[rolls eyes]* I don't even want to get into it.

See, here's the thing... I thought it was gonna be a drama-free year, right? Everything just smooth sailing. I'd be captain, most likely. I'd run a tight ship. The team would roll to the title. Easy, breezy, lemon squeezy.

Nope. Not even close. Pretty much non-stop drama right from the first day. New players. Fights. Season-ending injuries. Soccer's not hard enough? You gotta add drama? Crazy.

And I'd thought it would be so chill, you know? The easiest year ever. But what's that expression? *If you want to make God laugh, make a plan.* Something like that. Well, my plan was for a nice, easy year. And God was like, "Nope!" *[laughs]* "Hope you like chaos, Catalina!" *[laughs]*

Kaitlyn Baker, central midfielder: That was my senior year, but my first year at East. My parents were getting divorced and gave us the option of who we could live with. My brother stayed with Mom, but I moved in with my dad. And I moved solely for soccer. Solely so I could play for Carlos Orostieta. It was his last year, you know. He'd been coaching there for, what, thirty, forty years? He'd built East Sycamore into a juggernaut. Best program in the state. So yeah, it was an easy choice where to live. I chose completely and totally for soccer.

Granted, things weren't perfect. There were some tough times. Some injuries, some arguments, all that sort of thing. But that's part of soccer, isn't it? There's no such thing as a perfect season. Every team goes through ups and downs. That's part of the appeal, part of the reason we love it.

Was there a little extra drama that year? Maybe. Was I a part of it? Sure. Definitely. But would I change a minute of it? No. I loved that team. Loved that year. I'll never forget it.

Estefania Higuain, left back: That's a tough year to talk about. Not the soccer. The soccer was fine. But everything else?

[pauses]

That was the year my brother died.

I was a junior. Hugo would've been a senior, if he'd still been going to school. We'd moved to be closer to the hospital. I guess they specialized in bone cancer or something. That's what Hugo had. Bone cancer. So my parents moved us for that.

At first, I didn't think I'd go out for the team, but Hugo told me I had to. He loved soccer more than anything, and, you know, if he couldn't play, then I had to. That's what he told me.

The team itself, I didn't know much about them. They were supposed to be good, but that didn't matter. I wasn't really playing for wins and losses. I was playing for Hugo.

Chamique Lennox, backup goalkeeper: I wasn't even supposed to be on the team. Did you know that? Coach talked me into it.

He was my Spanish teacher. I was just this nobody kid. A freshman. Nobody at all. But I was tall. Only 5' 11" back then, but still growing. So one day in Spanish class, he asked if I play soccer.

I'd only played, like, one year in middle school. Goalie. But he was like, *Perfect, that's where I'd want you to play.*

I really didn't want to do it. Just the pressure, you know? I mean, the team was really, really good. And I'm supposed to back up Hayley Swanson? *The* Hayley Swanson? She was like a god at that school. She was tall and pretty, she played for the U18 National Team. Have you interviewed her yet? No? Well, that doesn't surprise me. She's pretty private. Maybe being a big star does that to you. Everybody wants a piece of you, so you protect yourself a little. I don't know.

Anyway, that was the situation. Coach was like, *Don't worry, you'll be the backup to the backup. Third string. No pressure at all.*

So, yeah. No pressure at all. And we know how that turned out, right?

Lisa Roney, center back: Oh, that was such a great year! I *loved* that team. Such a good bunch of girls. And Coach, I loved him. He's just the nicest guy. Have you talked to him yet? He's like your favorite grandfather. Crossed with Santa Claus. He's like a Latino Santa Claus grandfather. You can't help but love him.

That was my junior year. Catalina was next to me and we had a really good partnership. The team's offense was only so-so, but the defense? Me and Catalina in

the middle? Hayley Swanson in goal? Our fullbacks?
Man, what a defense!

There were some bumps in the road, sure. For me, for
the team. But maybe that's part of the reason I loved
that year. If it had been a smooth ride? If we'd cruised
the whole way? That's boring. Forgettable. But nope,
no smooth ride for us. Drama, right from the start.

Heck, I'd say the drama started first day, really, when
you think about Catalina and Kaitlyn.

West Sycamore High School

Nykesha Nolan, head coach: We were a couple weeks into school. I was doing the whole first-year teacher thing, getting my feet under me. Taught P.E., taught Health, it was all going pretty good. But, you know, as fun as teaching was, I was excited to start coaching. That's a lot of the reason I became a teacher; so I could coach.

I'd spent that whole summer trying to learn soccer. Coaching basketball? Softball? That was gonna be easy. I could run a basketball practice in my sleep. But soccer? What's a soccer practice even look like? I didn't know. What drills do you run? Do you scrimmage? Are there plays? Formations? I had to learn all that. I spent the whole summer learning. Getting ready.

When we finally had our first day of practice, I think I was more excited than the kids. A little nervous, sure, but mostly excited.

Susan Douglas, right winger: I was so glad when practice started up again. Soccer was my great escape back then. I'd been playing pickup soccer over the summer. There was a park near my grandma's house where I could get a game. Mostly adults. Mostly men. Latino, most of them. It was pretty weird, I'll admit, this little white girl running around with a bunch of fat, middle-aged Mexican guys, but I didn't care. I needed it. Especially that summer. That was a tough, tough summer.

Living with my grandma, that was normal. I'd been living with her a couple years, ever since Mom disappeared. She'd gotten back on the meth, disappeared. My dad... I didn't really have a dad. Never did. So Grandma, she was my family. That was my home. Not the best situation, but still, it was something.

And then, that summer – June, I think – the cops came by to tell us they'd found Mom's body. Some flop house a couple towns away. There was no funeral. She'd already been dead a few days when they found her.

You'd think something like that wouldn't have affected me too much, since she'd already been gone for so long, since she'd already been out of my life. But it did affect me. More than I expected. I guess having your mom die affects everyone, no matter the situation. I don't know.

Anyway, that's what I was dealing with that summer. And playing soccer in the park was the only time I felt halfway decent. I could just forget about life for awhile. So when school started, when practice started again, I was thrilled.

I didn't talk about any of this, so don't be surprised if the other girls don't know. Coach knew. The school knew. They kind of had to know, I guess. For legal reasons. But the team didn't. That was kind of my big thing back then; keeping it secret. Pretending to be normal.

It was lonely. You stay quiet, you keep secrets, you've got all this stuff going on in your life, and you can't talk about it with anyone. Very lonely.

But soccer? That was the best part of my life. The only good part, really.

Martha Sullivan, forward: Oh, yeah, I was super-excited for practice to start. I'd been running all summer, keeping myself in shape. I felt good. Felt like I was going to impress.

We were all excited to meet this new coach. Coach Nolan. Would she be any good? She was my Health teacher, so I already knew her. Liked her, too. But could she coach? No one knew. It made the start of practice even more exciting.

Clementine Thiamale, central defensive midfielder: I hadn't even met Coach yet, so when I showed up for that first day of practice, it was fun, wondering what she would be like.

[pauses]

It wasn't good.

That first practice, it was kind of a disaster, to be honest.

Maria Solana, central attacking midfielder: I could not wait for practice to start. I was wondering, *How do they do practices in America? Will it be different?* I was trying to be very open-minded.

On the practice field, we were all in this big circle, and Coach Nolan was talking. I was staying very close to the Latina girls, so they could translate for me. Coach Nolan would say something, one of the girls would whisper to me what she said. Coach Nolan would say something else, they would whisper it. And then it just kept going and going. She was talking, introducing herself, that sort of thing... and then she just kept talking and talking, and we were just standing there and standing there and I was thinking, *Are we ever going to play? Is this how they do it here? You just talk about soccer? You never play?*

Destinee Jones, left winger: God, that first day. She

just wouldn't shut up! *[laughs]* How long did we stand in that friggin' circle? Like, 45 minutes? *[laughs]* I'm not joking, it was forever!

It was her first year coaching, right? And I guess she was nervous or something, so she just kept talking and talking, on and on and on. "Here's what I think about soccer. Here's how we're gonna play. Here's what I expect from you." We're standing there with our cleats on, the sun beating down on us, this new lady droning on and on, and I sneak a peek at my watch and I'm like *Jeez O'Pete, practice time's almost over! Are we ever gonna play? [laughs]*

I think eventually we did some drills, but they were super, super simple. Like, 3rd grader drills. Just pee wee level stuff. We were all looking at each other, shaking our heads. I think someone – maybe Martha Sullivan – we passed each other doing this stupid 3rd grader drill and she was like, "Is this for real?" She said it really quiet. And I was like, "I don't know, man. I don't know."

This new lady, I knew it was her first year, so I wanted to be supportive, give her the benefit of the doubt and all that, but that first practice... it was demoralizing. We did that stupid drill for like five minutes or something, all of us rolling our eyes at each other, and then she's blowing her whistle, calling us all in.

She's like, "Okay, um, well, that's all we've got time for." And you could see in her eyes that she was embarrassed. Like, she knew she'd blown it. She'd blown her first practice. And I wasn't sure whether to feel bad for her, since she was new, or to be angry, since she was no better than the dope who'd coached us the year before. And I don't even remember his name. *[laughs]*

Afterward, we were all in the locker room, changing and stuff, and everyone was like, "What the hell? Is this what we've got to look forward to this year?" We were being all quiet about it, since, you know, she might have been right around the corner listening or something, but still, we weren't a happy crew. We were all like, *Welp, same ol', same ol' for West Sycamore. Another year going 7-7.*

Though, to be honest, at that point, seven wins seemed like a stretch. If we were gonna spend every practice standing in a circle, then doing some stupid pee wee drills, hell, we might not win a single game.

Nykesha Nolan, head coach: That was a tough night, lemme tell ya. I was a mess.

I was just so angry with myself, you know? So angry. I spent the whole summer thinking what a great coach I was going to be, so cocky, so sure I was going to kick ass, and then what happens? I go out on the first day and lay an egg. Completely blow it. I was devastated.

I actually called my college coach. My basketball coach, Katie Gillman. Called her that night, told her the whole story, told her how bad I'd screwed it up. Told her how the girls had been rolling their eyes, how they'd lost faith in me, how I wouldn't be able to win them back. I don't think I cried or anything, but I was definitely a mess. All that confidence I'd had? Completely gone.

She talked me off the ledge, though. Told me it wasn't over, that I hadn't lost the team forever. She was like, "It's not a sprint, Nykesha. It's a marathon. And you haven't even gone a quarter mile. This is the furthest thing from over."

We started talking about drills. Stuff I'd learned over the summer. Things I'd planned to do but hadn't. Coach Gillman, she wasn't a soccer coach, obviously, but it didn't matter. She knew how to run a practice. She knew how to lead a team.

I'd *thought* I knew how to do that stuff, but apparently not, right?

So she just talked about really basic stuff. First do this, then do this. She actually made me pull out a piece of paper and write it all down. One, start with this. Do it for five minutes, tops. Two, do this. How long on that? How long on the next thing? She had me write down a schedule for the entire practice.

It was incredibly helpful. By the time I hung up with her – I'm not sure how long we talked. Maybe an hour, maybe more – by the time we hung up, I was almost halfway optimistic. I was like, *Okay, tomorrow's gonna be better. I can do this. I can win them back. It's not a sprint, it's a marathon.*

But I'll be honest, going out there that second day, it was tough. Almost tougher than the first day. I won't lie, I was nervous as hell. But I had that schedule in my hand. I was prepared. It had to go better. It had to.

Clementine Thiamale, central defensive midfielder: The next day, Michelle and I were walking together out to the practice field. We were very nervous, wondering if it would be bad again. She was probably more discouraged than me. "Do I even want to be on the team?" she said. "If it's like that again? I'm not sure I do."

I was trying to be more positive, but it was tough. The whole team, we were very nervous going into that second practice. Very nervous.

But it was totally different. Coach Nolan, she was like a completely different person.

From the moment we got to the practice field, she had us moving. Blowing her whistle, yelling out orders, looking at her watch. "Go hard! Go hard!" That's the kind of thing she was yelling. "Keep it moving! Two minutes left! One minute left! Go hard!"

It was wonderful. So wonderful. And I wasn't the only one. We were all looking at each other with big eyes, big smiles.

"Next drill! Keep moving! Atta girl!" That was one of her favorite things to say. "Atta girl!" *[laughs]* I didn't even know what it meant at first. I understood *girl*, of course, but *atta*? I was asking the other girls, "What is *atta*? Is that a word?" *[laughs]*

So, yes, that second practice, everything turned around. Instead of wondering if this was going to be the worst year ever, instead of Michelle telling me she wasn't sure she wanted to be on the team anymore, suddenly we're all smiling and excited and thinking maybe this will be a good year after all, you know? It was wonderful.

Martha Sullivan, forward: God, you have no idea how glad I was. Because I was thinking about getting a scholarship, right? Score some goals, impress some colleges, get offered a scholarship? But you need, like, a functioning team to do that. With a competent coach. And practices where you actually *practice*.

So after that disaster of a first practice, I was like, *U.S. Army, here I come! Can't wait to start shooting those guns or... shooting those tanks or whatever.* Whatever Army people do.

Then, second day of practice comes, and everything changes. Suddenly we're a real soccer team with a real coach. And Coach Nolan, she was great from then on. That first day, that was the outlier. The lady who showed up the second day, that was the *real* Coach Nolan, the coach we had with us the rest of the year. Organized, energetic, fun. I grew to really like her. It was fun having a young coach who was excited and full of energy and pushing us to work hard.

As far as the rest of the team goes, it was a lot of the same girls as the year before. A few new ones. *[laughs]* Including one you might have heard of. Maria Solana? *[laughs]*

Susan Douglas, right winger: People ask me about her. We'll be watching the World Cup and Maria's on the TV, kicking ass, and my friends will be like, *You played with her? Seriously? What was she like? Was she awesome?*

I'll lie and pretend we were best friends. "Oh, yeah, BFFs." *[laughs]* "Super-close."

That second day of practice – the first day we actually did anything – that's when we finally got to see Maria do her thing. That's when everyone figured out, *Whoa, this new girl's really good.*

Destinee Jones, left winger: I'd seen her the first day. In the locker room, getting ready. She didn't look like anything special. Just your average girl. Average height, average weight. Nothing special at all.

She didn't speak English, really, so I asked this girl Yoreli about her. *[Yoreli Ospina, the team's right fullback]* Yoreli was like, "Oh, her name's Maria. She just moved here." I probably asked if she was Mexican or something and Yoreli was like, "No, she's Colombian."

And that was pretty much that. Some new girl from Colombia? Big deal.

But then that second day, when we finally started practicing for real, I was like, *Oh, hell. Maybe this* is *a big deal.*

Clementine Thiamale, central defensive midfielder: Maria's really famous now, of course, but ten years ago, she was nobody. Just another girl going out for the soccer team. I didn't know her at all. She was an immigrant, just like me the year before, so you would think we would know about each other, but we didn't. She lived in a different neighborhood, she spoke Spanish. There were lots of reasons we didn't know each other. But the first time we played together, none of that mattered. We started playing soccer, and it was so beautiful. She was a beautiful, beautiful player, even back then. All the things she does now, she did back then. Maybe they weren't as perfect as they are now, they weren't as polished, but it was all there. The skill was there. The beauty. We could all see it.

Maria Solana, central attacking midfielder: That first week of practice was very mixed for me. No, I guess what I really mean is, those first few weeks of *school* were mixed.

I told you that my family, we were taking English lessons. My parents, they really wanted us to be Americans. They talked about it all the time, about how if we worked hard, America would accept us. "America was built by immigrants," they would tell me and my sisters. "People just like us."

And then, in those first few weeks, we had a few people say some very ugly things to us. "Go back to Mexico. Quit stealing our jobs." Things like that. They would say it in English, so we didn't always understand it right away, but someone would translate it for us later. It was very upsetting.

It even happened to me at school. It was at this big meeting in the basketball gym. The whole school was there, all of us sitting in the stands. I was with some Latina girls that I was making friends with. And this American girl, too, I remember now. Well, I guess all the girls were American, but she was the only *white* girl sitting with us. Anyway, we were all there in the stands together and everyone was pressed in tight, the whole school, waiting for someone to talk. The principal, maybe. I don't remember what it was about.

There was this boy next to me. He was white. Very big. He looked at me and I smiled at him, trying to be nice, and he said some things to me in English. I didn't understand much of it, but it made the girls I was with very angry. All of them. The Latina girls, the white girl I told you about, they all got very angry and were yelling at him. He didn't seem to care.

I found out later – they wouldn't tell me everything he said – but it was something along the lines of, "Did you sneak over the border? Do you even speak English?" Things like that. Even without knowing the words, I could tell it was bad. I could see how he hated me. My friends, they defended me, of course, and that helped. Still, things like that, plus some other things that happened, things that happened to my parents, it was all very discouraging. It made me wonder if my parents were right to bring us from Colombia. Maybe America wouldn't accept us. Maybe we had made a mistake.

So that was in my mind a lot those first few weeks. Feeling very unsure.

Maybe that's why the soccer team became so important to me. Because that's where I felt like I most belonged. The girls, they accepted me. The white girls, the black girls, the Latina girls, everyone. They liked me. We were a big family. And I needed that.

Coach Nolan, she had that very bad first day of practice, but she turned out to be a wonderful coach. I liked her a lot, both as a coach and as a person.

Actually, I remember being very nervous at first. I thought Coach was frustrated by having to get the girls to translate for me. I remember asking them, "Is she mad at me?" and they were like, "No, no, you're fine, keep playing."

Destinee – you know Destinee Jones, right? – Destinee actually started to make a joke of it. *[laughs]* A running joke, I think it's called. She would accuse the Latina girls of telling me the wrong thing. Telling me silly things, just to be funny. You know, telling me to pick my nose or something. *[laughs]* "Stop telling her to pick her nose! How dare you!" *[laughs]* Destinee was so funny. I liked her very much.

I don't know if you've ever been in a situation like that, but it's funny when someone's telling jokes in a different language, because you know they're being funny, you just don't know what they're saying. And all around you, the whole team is laughing, and you can tell they're not laughing at *you*, they're just laughing. And because they're all laughing and having fun, you start laughing, too. You just have no idea what you're laughing at, because it's all in English. In the end, though, you don't really care. It just feels good to be laughing and feeling like you're surrounded by friends. Destinee was good at that. She was good at making us feel like a big group of friends. A family, really.

I needed that. There were a lot of difficult things that year, a lot of times I wondered if I could ever become an American. But never with the team. The soccer team, that was where I always felt I belonged.

Destinee Jones, left winger: Damnation, could that little girl play some soccer. Seriously. She comes in, I think she was a junior, brand new to America, spoke pretty much zero English, and damn if she didn't just kick everyone's ass, right from day one.

Funny thing is, at first, the soccer was kind of ugly. She was playing beautifully, but the rest of the team, me included, we weren't at her level *at all*. So it took us a few days to kind of... get in sync, I guess. Like, if our first real practice was on Tuesday, Maria was out there kicking ass and the rest of us were just kind of watching her with our mouths hanging open, like, *Dude, this chick is amazing.* That kind of thing. We were actually saying that to each other. But it wasn't until Thursday or Friday that we got over it, pulled our big mouths closed, and started figuring out how to play with her.

And when that happened, when we all started working together, oh, hell fire, it was nice. It was honestly the first time I'd ever been like, *Oh, this is why they call it the beautiful game.* When we all started figuring each other out, started working together like we could, it really was beautiful. I'd liked soccer up until then, but that was the first year I loved it.

Martha Sullivan, forward: At a certain point during those first couple weeks, I started thinking, *Could we actually be* good *this year?*

I'm not sure what day it was... third day? Fourth? It was toward the end of practice, we'd been doing drills and stuff, and Coach finally let us play a quick scrimmage. I'll never forget it. 11v11. Game to three. First team to score three goals wins.

You figure three goals should take awhile, right? Nope. Maria scored twice in, like, 90 seconds, then fed someone else for the third goal right after that. It was insane. She was just head and shoulders above everyone else.

I wasn't on her team for that scrimmage, but it didn't matter. I remember being super-excited, thinking, *Oh, wow, we* are *gonna be good. This new girl, she's gonna crush teams.*

30

But then I started to get a little nervous, you know? I was thinking, *Am I good enough? Am I going to let her down?*

It's funny, looking back on it. She's this brand new girl, doesn't know anyone, doesn't speak English, but I'm the one trying not to let *her* down.

Nykesha Nolan, head coach: I'm not sure when I figured out how good we were. Not immediately. Remember, I was still figuring out soccer myself. If it had been basketball or softball, I would have been totally comfortable. I would've seen it all right away. But that year, soccer was still new, so I was kind of learning on the fly.

Obviously the most significant player was Maria Solana. She *was* that team, plain and simple. Running things from the middle of the field, controlling the game, making the passes. What did she have that year, 17 goals, 20 assists? Something ridiculous like that. And that's in 13 games, not 14, because she missed that one game. Won state player of the year in a landslide. It may have been unanimous, I can't remember. It should've been.

Our wingers were good. Destinee Jones on the left, Susan Douglas on the right. Destinee played her tail off. Just non-stop effort, offense and defense, the whole game. Good kid. Played hard, always joking around, good kid.

Susan Douglas, over on the other wing... Susan had a hard life. She was going through a lot of stuff that year. I'm not going to tell you about it. Maybe she will. Let's just say she kept a lot of stuff to herself. As a player, though? Very good. Great foot skills. Could dribble like no one's business. Probably the second-best passer on the team, after Maria. I could've used a bit more aggressiveness from her, but talent-wise, she was excellent.

We had a couple strikers. Daniela DeLeon, she was pretty good, but the one who really took off that year was Martha Sullivan. Little waterbug of a girl. Tiny. Maybe five feet tall, a hundred pounds soaking wet. I remember, at first, thinking she'd just get run over out there, but she was so damn quick, so damn shifty. Constantly moving. Scored a lot of goals for us that year.

We were an offensive team, but if there was one defensive player to mention, it's Clementine Thiamale. Short girl, big smile, tough as nails. Super-popular with the rest of the team. Everyone loved Clementine. She'd set up right in front of the back line and put out a lot of fires for us. Almost a third center back, really. Only short.

What was it Destinee used to say? She had this little Clementine chant she'd sometimes do in practice. Clem would knock someone down, steal the ball, and Destinee would start chanting, "She's short! She's hard! She's got a yellow card! She's Clem! She's Clem! She's Clemmmmmmmmmmmm!" Something like that.

It was funny. Like I said, everyone loved Clementine. Great kid.

Destinee Jones, left winger: Lemme tell you about this one play, and I know it sounds stupid that I would remember one play from this one practice way back in high school, but seriously, this was when I fell in love with soccer.

It was a scrimmage. 11v11. It was probably Monday or Tuesday of that second week. Coach hadn't really figured out her starters, so we're all mixed together. I was on Maria's team. So was Martha Sullivan. Clementine was on the other team, playing D.

By this point, I think we'd all figured out, *Oh, man, this year, it ain't like last year. We could actually be good.* And that realization changed everything. The practices got serious. Players were really getting after it. Girls were really sweating, trying to keep up with Maria. I was no different. I was out there like, *Don't let her down. She's gonna slip you a pass. Don't mess it up.* It was crazy. And awesome. It was all the things.

So we're having this scrimmage and I'm on Maria's team, which means we're winning. But Clementine's on the other team, which means their defense isn't gonna go down without a fight, right? Clem's out there banging, shutting down attacks, knocking people on their butts. You know, Clem stuff.

Anyway, I've got the ball. I'm on the left and Maria's in the middle. Clementine's there, too, kind of lurking, so

I know if I pass it to Maria, Clem's gonna shut her down. Try to, at least. But earlier that day – I probably should have started the story with this – earlier that day, we'd been working on the give-and-go. You know, pass it to someone, immediately run to some open space, and get the ball passed back to you. Basic stuff, sure, but remember, this is high school. You work on the basics. Some of those things, you're still figuring out. Anyway, Maria, she'd been super helpful with all that. Almost like a second coach. She had one of the Latina girls translating for her – Yoreli or Daniela or someone – and she and I had really nailed the whole give-and-go thing.

Okay, back to the scrimmage. I'm on the left, coming down the side, and I'm like, *You know what, let's do this.* So as soon as my defender comes up on me, I slip Maria the pass and sprint for the end line. Well, no surprise, she one-times it back to me and I've got the ball in acres of empty space.

Okay, so great story, right? It gets better.

I start cutting in toward goal, totally free, and Clementine sees me. She's like, *Oh, hell, I better put a stop to this*, because, you know, that's what Clem did. But just as she's coming up on me, ready to blow me up, I see little Martha Sullivan sitting there in the box and I'm like, *Why not? Let's try it again.*

So I slip Martha the ball, keep running, and sure enough, just as the defense is collapsing on her, she taps the ball back to me, I've got a full head of steam, and I one-time it straight into the back of the net.

Oh, Lord have mercy, did I scream. I was jumping up and down, grabbing Martha and Maria and, hell, I would've grabbed Clementine if she'd been close enough. I was just so happy.

This sounds dumb, doesn't it? Some stupid little give-and-go in a stupid little scrimmage ten years ago. But, honestly, that play right there, that's when I fell in love with soccer. That's when I figured it all out. I was like, *Oh, I get it. Soccer's beautiful. Soccer's fun. Soccer makes sense.*

That switch didn't get flipped until I was a senior in high school, and it probably never *would* have been flipped without Maria Solana and Nykesha Nolan, but whatever. It happened, that's all that matters.

By the end of those two weeks of preseason, I think everyone on the team knew, *We ain't going 7-7 again. Everything's changed.*

East Sycamore High School

Estefania Higuain, left back: Those first few weeks of school were hard. Moving to a new school is tough. Pretty much all of it. You don't know anybody, you don't know your way around. *Where are my classes? Where's the cafeteria?* Everything's just a little harder than it was at your old school. Plus, you're a little lonely. You don't have any friends.

And then there was life at home. Hugo's health was very poor. He was seeing new doctors at this new hospital, they were trying new things, things he wasn't used to. His body didn't always have a good reaction and he'd have to spend a few nights at the hospital. It was tough on everyone. Hugo most of all.

To be honest, I really did wonder if the soccer team was

just something I couldn't do. Life was so busy, you know? New school, new people, new everything. When school let out, maybe I was going home or maybe I was going to the hospital to see Hugo. There was just so much... chaos? I don't think that's the right word. Not chaos. But something like that. Life was just too much. So, would I go out for the soccer team? I really wasn't sure.

But like I told you, in the end, Hugo decided it. He said I had to. I had to go out for the team and then give him a report every day. He was very clear on that. Every day, he wanted a report.

I'm glad he made me join the team. It was good for me. Kind of the only normal thing in my life, I guess.

But was I excited about practices starting? Hard to say. It was mixed. Everything was mixed that year.

Carlos Orostieta, head coach: Oh yes, I was very excited for the first week of practice. Very excited. I knew how good the team would be. I knew the quality of players who were coming back. Roney, Forero, and Hayley Swanson? With that kind of talent, how could I not be excited?

I remember telling myself, *Carlito, this year, you must win it all. It is your final year. You have so much talent on the team. You must win it all. You must!*

That sort of pressure, even from within – *especially* from within – well, it is difficult. It can make the game a little less enjoyable. And it really is a game, you know. It should be fun. But with that sort of talent, you do feel the pressure to win.

So yes, to answer your question, I was glad when practice finally began. My last team. Would it be my greatest team? No way to say yet. But when you step out there on the practice field at the start of the year, it's always nice. Very nice. Like magic. The smell of the grass, the sound of the balls being kicked back and forth, all of those players running around, looking to you, wondering what sort of coach you are, what sort of season this will be.

Ah, I miss it sometimes. I do. Yes, the pressure was high, but maybe that was part of the fun.

Kaitlyn Baker, central midfielder: Are you kidding? I couldn't *wait* for practice to start. Those first couple weeks of school, I was going crazy waiting for it.

Starting at a new school is difficult. I mean, I didn't have any *big* problems or anything, but still, it was tough. More annoying than tough, I guess. It's just... I was a senior, right? And as a senior, you're supposed to be top of the food chain and all that. But when you're brand new and don't know anyone, don't have any friends, you're sort of like a freshman. Those first couple weeks, I remember being very aware of how much easier life would have been if I'd stayed at my old school. But like I said, I was at East for the soccer program.

I'd gone and found Coach in his classroom, introduced myself. You know, just to let him know who I was. Let him know I was serious. I'd had a little contact with other players on the team, but not a huge amount. Not enough to develop relationships or anything. By the time that first practice rolled around, I was beyond pumped. Walking into that locker room first day, I was practically vibrating, I was so pumped up. I definitely hit the ground running.

Lisa Roney, center back: Oh yeah, I noticed Kaitlyn, right from the start. Even in the locker room beforehand, you couldn't miss her. Super vocal. Introducing herself to everyone. Not acting at all like a new girl. "Alright, girls. This is our year." That's how she was talking. "Let's get off to a good start today." Stuff like that.

I was listening to it, thinking, *Who is this crazy girl, coming in here like she owns the place?*

Catalina was even worse. She was changing next to me and I remember her rolling her eyes at me. Just looking really annoyed by it. We hadn't even made it out to the practice field yet, and already there were problems.

Catalina Forero, center back: Yeah, Kaitlyn put me right on edge. Instantly.

See, here's the thing. We had an established team. We had seniors. We had leaders. Me and Hayley, one of us would be captain. Probably me, really. Hayley's a little too quiet. But still, the two of us, we were gonna

39

run that team. We were gonna set the tone. Set the culture.

Then suddenly this new chick shows up out of nowhere, acting like she's in charge? Walking around the locker room, clapping her hands, introducing herself, giving pep talks? Are you kidding me? I friggin' hated her, right from the start.

So there I was, wondering how to handle it. Lisa's there, she's always so chill. Hayley, too. Hayley's a leader, sure, but she's a quiet leader. She's got a quiet strength.

But this new chick was so vocal, so energetic, and I was like, *Okay, I gotta match this. I gotta bring my energy up, show the team who's boss.* So there I was, getting all pumped up and loud. Clapping my hands and whatnot.

The whole thing felt weird, you know? It felt like I was forcing it. Changing my style. Being somebody I wasn't. And why? Because this stupid new girl I've never seen before thinks she's something special? Why should I have to change for her? She should have to change for me.

So yeah, first day, first time walking out to the practice field, and I was already pissed off. Already sick of Kaitlyn.

Chamique Lennox, backup goalkeeper: I was so nervous that first practice. *So* nervous. I'm not sure I said two words the entire time. I mostly watched Hayley Swanson. I was kind of in awe of her. The whole school was, really. And now I was on the same team as her? Playing the same position? It was insane. I was terrified.

The second-string keeper was a girl named Ruthann Arquin. She was nice. I wasn't afraid to talk to her. If we were gonna do keeper drills or something, I'd be off to the side, all scared and everything, watching Hayley, asking Ruthann what I was supposed to do. I was probably whispering to her, afraid Hayley would hear me. It's crazy. Hayley was just *so* intimidating.

So yeah, I was quiet that first practice. That whole first week, I'm sure.

I noticed Lisa, though. Lisa Roney. She was so hot. I couldn't take my eyes off her.

I wasn't out, back then. I knew I was gay, but I'd never said anything to anyone. I was still getting used to it myself, you know? But Lisa, she was out.

She was a junior. I knew about her, I'd seen her in the halls. She had this great hairdo. Short. Kind of a pixie cut, I guess, but bleached super super blond. Really hot.

So yeah, I spent a lot of that first practice checking her out. Watching her out the corner of my eye, trying to be all super-secret about it.

Lisa Roney, center back: Yeah, I noticed Chamique. She was cute as hell. Really shy, really awkward. She was a freshman, you know. Looked it, too. Skinny. All knees and elbows. But cute. Really cute. I saw her over there with Hayley, trying to be invisible. Trying to watch me without getting caught. It was cute.

But in truth, cute freshman girls eyeing me from the sideline was kind of the last thing on my mind that first week of practice. The main thing was Kaitlyn and Catalina. God almighty, those two.

Catalina Forero, center back: I'm not sure when we first blew up at each other. Was it first day? It might have been. She just drove me insane, you know? Clapping her hands, yelling all the time. "Here we go, girls! Here we go!" Stuff like that. Drove me friggin' crazy.

Hayley didn't like it much, either, but it affected her a little less, you know? She was in goal, not out in the field. She had a little bit of separation. And anyway, Hayley was just naturally more chill.

But me, I was right there in the middle of it. Coach had Kaitlyn playing central midfield, right in front of me and Lisa. So I couldn't escape her, you know?

I'd always thought I was a pretty good leader. Always thought I was pretty vocal, keeping the back line organized, that sort of thing. But now Kaitlyn comes along and she won't shut up. We're running drills, she's talking. We're playing a scrimmage, she's barking out orders. It was non-friggin'-stop.

I was a senior, I knew the team, I'd done my time. Now this new girl shows up and wants to take over? I was *not* cool with that. Not at all.

Kaitlyn Baker, central midfielder: What was I supposed to do? Catalina wasn't vocal enough. She just wasn't. The team needed direction. It needed a leader. There was a void, I filled it. Catalina didn't like it? Fine. I wasn't there to make friends. I was there to win.

Estefania Higuain, left back: Hugo *loved* the Kaitlyn/Catalina stories. *Loved* them.

I told you how he wanted daily reports. I'd come home and he'd be like, "Tell me everything." That first day, after the very first practice, he was like, "Who are the players? How is the coach? What position did you play? What drills did you run?" He couldn't get enough.

And, without a doubt, the number one thing he loved? Kaitlyn and Catalina wanting to kill each other.

When did they first blow up? I think it was in the locker room after that first practice. Catalina kind of kept her cool out on the practice field – *kind of* – but then in the locker room, she finally let Kaitlyn have it. Told her to shut up, probably. I can't remember the exact fight, the exact words, but they fought. And trust me, that was only the first one, it certainly wasn't the last. And Hugo, he ate it up. He loved it. I didn't really root for either Kaitlyn or Catalina to win. I didn't care who ended up being captain. But Hugo, he was definitely Team Kaitlyn. He loved the idea of this new girl coming in and taking over. Loved it.

Truth is, I may have played up the fights a little bit for him. His life was so bad those days. In pain from the cancer, sick from the treatments. My soccer stories were one of the only good things in his life, really. So when I saw how much he liked the Kaitlyn/Catalina drama, I may have played it up a little. Spent a little extra time describing it. Maybe added a little here and there. It was fun.

But, you know, it's not like I was inventing it out of thin air. It was real. They didn't like each other.

Carlos Orostieta, head coach: Oh, yes, my friend, it was real. There was real trouble between those two, no doubt. But that is part of coaching, isn't it? It is not all x's and o's. It's not all game plans and formations and all of that. A big part of coaching is managing personalities. Sometimes it seemed like that was the *biggest* part. That year, it certainly did.

I did what I could, of course. I spoke to the girls, tried to work things out. But in some ways, these are things players must work out themselves. Does the coach really choose the captain? Or does the captain choose herself?

So those first few weeks, sometimes I kept the peace,

and sometimes I did not. Sometimes I stepped aside and let the girls work things out themselves. Because maybe that is when the real captain shows herself. Maybe that's when we figure out who will lead the team.

Kaitlyn Baker, central midfielder: It took awhile. Catalina, man, she wasn't going down without a fight. And good on her, right? Good on her. She should fight. That's what a team needs. Fighters. So did I mind the fights? The tension? God, no. I wanted the tension. That's how championships are won.

Catalina Forero, center back: Of course she liked it. She's a fighter. That's, like, the one-word description of Kaitlyn Baker. Fighter.

Me? I didn't like it as much. Not at the time. I was talking with Hayley, talking with Lisa, and they were supportive. They were, like, "Keep working, man. Coach knows you. He knows what you bring to the team."

I wanted that friggin' arm band, you know? I wanted to be captain. And it's almost like having Kaitlyn come in and push me like she did, that made me want it more. Before practice started, I'd just assumed I'd get the arm band. Like it was a given. Now, who knew? Maybe me. Maybe Kaitlyn. Hell, maybe Coach would just give it to Hayley, just to shut me and Kaitlyn up. I had no idea. I just knew it was important now. It was no longer just an assumed thing. If I was gonna be captain, I'd have to earn it.

Kind of made it more fun, in a way. More meaningful, at least.

Lisa Roney, center back: That first week of practice, I could tell Chamique wanted to talk to me, but was afraid to. I could see her checking me out, pretending she *wasn't* checking me out, that sort of thing. I started talking to her a little. You know, just asking how she was doing, how the whole goalkeeper thing was working out. Safe stuff.

Chamique Lennox, backup goalkeeper: I couldn't tell if she liked me or not. I mean, she was being friendly and all, but did that mean she liked me? Maybe she was just being friendly. Just being nice to this dumb freshman girl pretending she was a goalie.

I think it was after practice that first Friday, she was like, "Hey, me and some friends are getting coffee tomorrow. You wanna join us?"

God, I almost fainted, I was so excited. I was thinking, *Omigod, coffee! With friends! Who are they? Gay friends? Does she know I'm gay? She can't. How could she? What should I wear? What do people wear to coffeeshops? Should I try and look gay? What does that even mean? How do you look gay?* It was terrifying and wonderful and I could barely sleep Friday night thinking about it.

Lisa Roney, center back: It was a bunch of my gay friends. Like, four or five of us. I was like, *Oh, this'll* *be a nice thing I can do for Chamique. Get her around some gay folks, let her see it's not so scary. It'll be good for her.*

And it was. We were all just hanging out, drinking coffee and talking. Not about anything important. Just stuff. It was pretty chill.

Chamique was quiet at first, but then she started to relax and join the conversation and enjoy herself.

And it was weird... at a certain point, I was like, *Wow, Chamique's totally cool.* I mean, I genuinely liked her. I was enjoying her company.

Afterwards, people were taking off and the whole thing was breaking up, and I asked Chamique what she had planned for the day and she was like, "Nothing. This. I guess I'll go home."

Somehow we both decided we didn't really want to go home yet, so there was this movie theater there, one of those smaller theaters that show older movies, so we decided to go see a movie. And then after that we did something else and then something else and before you knew it, it was a real live date.

Crazy, right? Last thing I expected, falling for some little freshman girl. But there you are. Our first date.

West Sycamore High School

Nykesha Nolan, head coach: After two weeks, it was time for our first game. I was really nervous. Really uncertain. I liked what I'd seen in practice, I thought the girls played well together, but you know, how did we compare to other teams? I had no idea.

Our first game was against... who was it against? I can't even remember.

Destinee Jones, left winger, team captain: First game was against Yellow Springs. A road game. Maybe 30 minutes down the road in Jefferson. We played them every year and they'd always been kind of like us. A fairly middling team.

I was so excited going into that game. I knew we'd

crush 'em. I think I was the only one willing to say it out loud. Everyone else was like, *Oh, you know, we won't really know until we play a real game*, and I was like, *Whatever*. I'd been on that team three years. I knew what a normal West Sycamore team looked like. This team was head and shoulders above that. Yeah, sure, it was just practice, but who cares? The difference in quality was obvious. A blind man could see how much better we were.

The bus ride there was pretty chill. It usually is on the way to games. The bus ride home, that's either happy or sad, depending on the result, but the bus ride *to* games, that's usually somewhere in between. Everybody's getting their game face on.

I was wearing the captain's armband that day. That was awesome. I knew I had a pretty good chance to win it, but still, actually having Coach give it to me was pretty fabulous. I remember it so well. Feeling it on my bicep. Trying to figure out where to put it. Left arm? Right arm? On my sleeve or on my skin? If I put it on my skin, will my sleeve come down and cover it up? If I put it on my sleeve, will it be too tight? Will that annoy me? Will the sleeve rub my arm too much? You know, all the dumb little things you don't think about until you're actually having to deal with them.

Nykesha Nolan, head coach: I was *so* nervous. My first soccer game. My first time being a coach in *any* sport. First time shaking the opposing coach's hand. First time shaking the referee's hand. Handing him the lineup card. So many firsts.

I'd actually called Katie Gillman the night before. You know, my college coach? I didn't want to mess up my first game like I did that first day of practice. She was awesome, though. We made another list. Do this, do this, don't forget this. Dang, she helped me so much.

You know, you think you're ready, you think you're gonna be the greatest coach ever, but then when the moment comes, you're scared. It's a good kind of scared, I guess, but still. I didn't want to mess anything up.

So anyway, all the pregame stuff's taken care of, the girls are out there on the field, and the ref blows his whistle. Actually, I think it was a she that day. I'm not sure. It doesn't matter. So the ref blows her whistle and play starts and I'm on the sideline trying not to hyperventilate. I'm like, *Okay, Nykesha. Now you get to see if your team's any good.*

Destinee Jones, left winger, team captain: We killed them. 3-1. And that score makes it seem closer than it really was. We put a couple shots off the post, another couple off the crossbar. I think Maria put one or two right into the goalkeeper's belly. Honestly, that game could have been 7-1. 8-1. It was a complete blowout.

During the game, I didn't quite know how to handle it. I was just giddy with how we were playing, practically skipping down the field, laughing, cheering, just this huge smile on my face. And I was like, *Wait, hold on. Maybe this isn't how you handle a blowout win.*

[laughs] I didn't know. I'd never had to deal with it before. And here I was, the captain. I knew I was supposed to set the example. So that was weird. Trying to figure out how to behave when you're killing a team. How to be a good winner. I don't know if I did such a good job of it that day. I was too happy. Too shocked.

But I got better at it. There were a lot more victories to come.

Martha Sullivan, forward: I scored two goals in the first game! That was my total for the entire previous season! Next game, I had another goal. Third game, another. It was crazy.

Remember, I'd wanted to score a little more that year, hoping for a scholarship. Then when I bagged two in that first game, I was like, *Holy crap, this could actually happen. I could actually get recruited.* So, thank you, God, for sending me Maria Solana.

Maria Solana, central attacking midfielder: Martha Sullivan was our striker. She was a nice girl. Small. Fast. A hard worker. She played like a slippery little fish. She was not big, so she had to find empty places. Make the defenders forget where she was. And she was very good at that. I think we worked well together, me and Martha.

Clementine Thiamale, central defensive midfielder: The whole offense worked well together. They clicked right from the start. Maria, Martha, Destinee, Susan

Douglas, Daniela DeLeon. They were amazing. Maria Solana was the key, of course. She made everyone better.

I didn't really move forward too much. Mostly I stayed back on defense, watching for counter attacks. Tried to stop them before they could really get started. I enjoyed it. Coach Nolan, she told me to be more aggressive. That was a big thing that year. Be aggressive. Act. Don't wait for the other team to act. Make them react to you.

She had this thing she would say to us before every game. She would say, "First tackle, first foul, first shot, first goal." She wanted us to be the first for everything. Don't wait for the other team. Do it first. "First tackle, first foul, first shot, first goal."

Nykesha Nolan, head coach: I stole that from Bruce Arena, the old U.S. national coach. I borrowed stuff from all over. He's a pretty good coach to steal ideas from.

Maria Solana, central attacking midfielder: I did not know if we were a good team. Not right away. Part of that was being new to America. Maybe it is like that for all immigrants. You know how things were in your old country, but in your new country? You are not sure. *Are we a good team? We are winning, but I am still not sure.*

Everything in life was a little strange back then. My town in Colombia was very small. Just a village, really.

So I come to America and the town is bigger, the school is bigger, the *people* are bigger. *[laughs]* I liked the changes, they were exciting, but sometimes it was overwhelming.

I've lived in three countries now, and I can tell you, when you move to a new country, there are all these little differences, little tiny things that throw you off. The grocery store is different. Going to a restaurant is different. The milk you get, it is just a little different. Going to the movies. Things like that.

And I guess soccer was the same. I knew the teams in my tiny little part of Colombia, but in America? What's a good team look like in America?

Then we started winning and winning and winning. After maybe three or four games where we won by a big score, I started to figure it out. *Oh, this is what teams are like here. And we are really good.*

It was a nice feeling. A nice discovery. It is like when a girl realizes, *Oh, I am actually pretty?* Or, I suppose, when a boy is like, *Oh, I am handsome? Girls like me?* That is what it was like. *Oh, my team is very good? How exciting!*

Destinee Jones, left winger, team captain: Yeah, we were good. Hella good. We weren't just winning, we were winning big. 3-1, 4-1, 5-2. It was so much fun.

My family actually started coming to games. Well, my mom. The rest of them, they didn't care about soccer. I told you, we were a football family. Dad played in college. My brothers all played. They were stars, really. My older brother Michael was playing at Fresno State. Zak, he was a year below me, he was the starting running back. James, he was a wide receiver. They both went on to play in college. So we weren't just *sort of* a football family. It was a big, big deal.

What did they think of me playing soccer? They didn't. At all. *[laughs]* I think my mom had been to a game the year before. Maybe James had come at some point. Maybe. But my dad? God, no. He couldn't have cared less. I might as well have been doing... I don't know... ballet. That's how much my family cared about soccer.

But then, that year, we were suddenly good – suddenly *great* – and people were talking. Around school, there was just the tiniest of buzzes about the team. My brothers were like, "What's up with you guys? Did you really win a game 7-2?" And I'm like, "Yeah, we're good now, you should come watch us play."

They didn't come right away. Mom came to a game. The boys were in the middle of football season. Dad didn't care. But, you know, Mom came to that one game and was impressed. She told everyone about it, said we were the real deal. I figured that was a good start. Maybe if we kept winning, the guys would come, too.

Maria Solana, central attacking midfielder: I remember some of the girls were talking about how we could win State. I did not know what they were talking about. My little school in Colombia, yes, we had a team, a small team, but it wasn't quite the same. There was no state championship, not like they have in America. The whole thing is organized differently. So I did not really know what the girls were talking about, not at first. But everyone was saying we had a chance to win State and I could tell that was a good thing, so I got excited for it, even though I didn't really know what it meant.

My best friend on the team was Yoreli Ospina, the right back. My English was very poor that first year, and Yoreli was a big help. She translated for me. She helped me with my English lessons. She said that she liked doing it, which is good. Yoreli was a good friend. I needed friends that year.

I told you earlier about that boy in the gymnasium. The one who said the things to me, who told me to go home. There were others. Not a lot. I don't want you to think everyone was mean to me. They weren't. But some were. Some people at school, some people outside of school. My parents, my sisters, we all have stories we could tell you. People who treated us badly.

And then there were the people who were wonderful to me. All the people who wanted to help me. Yoreli. Coach Nolan. The people in my neighborhood.

The old lady at the church giving English lessons? She didn't get paid, she did it for free. I remember asking her, "Were you an immigrant? Is that why you help us?"

She said she wasn't. "My grandparents were, years and years ago." That is what she said. I think she said they were from Germany or Russia or somewhere. "It was hard for them," she said. "People didn't always welcome them. Didn't always want to help them. If I can make it a little easier for you, then I will." That is what she said. I remember it. She was a good person. There were many good people. A few bad ones, but many more who were good.

I think you have spoken to Clementine Thiamale? She was an immigrant. Not that year with me, but the year before. She came from Africa and spoke French.

Clementine was such a nice girl. She had this big, big smile. Everyone loved her. And she was an important player for us, also. She played defensive midfield. Our defense was not as strong as our offense, but Clementine was a very good player. She was very good at stopping attacks before they made it to our back line. A very good player. Very high energy, very strong. What is the word in English, when you never stop trying? Tenacious? Yes. That was Clementine. She was tenacious. I liked Clementine as a player and I also liked that she was an immigrant like me.

Clementine Thiamale, central defensive midfielder: I told you how hard it was the year before, my first year in America, but my second year, things got better. My English got better and I realized I was starting to get closer to people. It's a slow process, making friends. It's slow for anyone, I guess, but especially when you're doing it in a different language. But that second year, things got better. I started feeling like my friends were real friends. Like my teammates were real teammates. Like I belonged there. I stopped feeling like a new kid. Like an immigrant. I started to feel a little like an American.

Oh, and that was also the year I got my first boyfriend. That was nice. *[laughs]* I can't believe I'm blushing, it was so long ago. Still, at the time it was very scary and very exciting and wonderful. I guess it's like that for everybody.

His name was Curtis. Curtis Wallace. He was a junior, same as me. Very cute. Very nice. He was short, like me. I loved his eyes. There were so many things I liked about him. Maybe that's how it is for everyone and their first boyfriend. You forget the bad things, you just look back on the excitement and the confusion and the fun of it all.

You can see how it was an exciting year for me. Starting to make close friends, starting to feel like I belonged, plus I get my first boyfriend. *And* the team is suddenly so good? It was an exciting year. Really, it's one of my favorite years ever.

Susan Douglas, right winger: The team looked great, right from the start. The offense especially. We won our first... heck, how many games did we win to start the year? 10? 11? 12? It was so different, being on a really good team. So new.

I could only halfway enjoy it. The other girls were having a blast, all smiles and laughter and whatnot, but my life was only getting worse.

I told you my mother died in June. Well, in September, my grandma joined her. Not a meth overdose, of course. Just being old. Died in her sleep.

It still hurts, ten years later. That whole year... honestly, I don't know how I survived it. Only seventeen years old and I had to go through all that. My husband tells me how strong I must have been, and I guess that's true, but I didn't always feel it, not at the time. I just felt like this kid who the universe was beating the crap out of day after day after day.

I went through a series of foster homes. It's hard to remember them all, but there were a bunch. I'd spend two weeks in one place – it might be okay, it might be awful – then they'd move me to another place. Again, it might be awful, it might be fine – and then another place. Coach Nolan knew about all of it, but otherwise, I didn't tell a soul. I didn't tell Coach, either. It was the office telling her. She'd check on me, ask me if I was okay, if I needed anything, but I told her right from the start that I didn't want anyone else knowing. And she was cool about that. She kept my secret.

I look back on that, wondering what would have happened if I'd let people know. If I'd let down my guard. How would they have reacted? Would it have been better for me? Worse? Would I have been a little less lonely? It's tough carrying all that inside you, never letting anyone help you carry the burden. I can see that now, but ten years ago? No. I was just a kid trying to survive. Trying to pretend I was normal.

Martha Sullivan, forward: So, the winning continued. Once a team gets a little momentum, you get hard to stop. I really believe that. If we lose our first game? Our second game? We probably would've figured, *Oh, we're just the same old West Sycamore.* But win our first five, six, seven games? And win them handily? Everyone starts to believe. You start to think you can't lose.

The goals kept coming. How many goals did I have that year? 12? 13? Just shy of a goal a game, I think. It was insane.

We were definitely an offensive team. Offense was the big story. Our defense? Nothing special. I think we had maybe one shutout the whole year. But that was okay. As much as we scored, if the D could keep it low, just give up one goal, maybe two, we were probably winning. That's how we looked at it.

Nykesha Nolan, head coach: Like I've said, I was still figuring out how to coach soccer, so in a way, playing fast, that was easier. Having an air-tight defense, that's a tougher thing to do. Carlos Orostieta, he had an air-tight D. Absolutely bulletproof. But he'd been doing it for 30, 40 years. He knew what he was doing. Me? I was still learning.

But let me tell you one of the keys of coaching. I've

figured this out over time. First and foremost, figure out what kind of players you've got, then plan your tactics around that. Got a bunch of big tough girls? Play big tough girl soccer. Got a bunch of girls who can run? Turn 'em loose. Run like hell. Got a creator like Maria Solana?

[laughs]

But, of course, how many coaches have got a creator like Maria Solana? Like I said, I was probably the luckiest first-year coach ever.

Destinee Jones, left winger, team captain: Yeah, we were just pedal to the metal, all the time. Though, you know, we did have a defensive strategy, it just wasn't a sit-back-and-shut-things-down sort of strategy. Just the opposite. Coach wanted us to press. High pressure from the start of the game to the finish. Get turnovers high up the field, turn 'em into goals.

Little Martha Sullivan was great at that. That girl had a *motor*. Never stopped running.

Martha Sullivan, forward: I liked it. It's fun harassing defenders when they have the ball. Because, you know, they're already big and clumsy. And now they've got me racing up, trying to take the ball? They can't handle it. Harass the goalkeeper, harass the center backs, get them to make a bad pass. I loved it. Destinee and I both did well at it. We both liked to run. And when you get turnovers way up the field like that, you're already in a good position to score. Which we did.

I can't remember when I got my first recruitment letter. Six games into the season? It was from Purdue University. I'll never forget it. Purdue. My second letter was from Georgia Tech. The third was Colorado State. There were others, too, trickling in. They were all just preliminary letters, just showing interest, but oh my, was I excited. I remember putting them up on my wall.

I called the schools, talked to the coaches. They were a little unsure about me, since I'd only just started scoring goals in my senior year, but still, they were intrigued. They told me to keep up the good work, keep doing well, and at the end of the season, maybe we could talk about scholarship opportunities.

Well, you can imagine, I was over the moon. Just beside myself. I had a million thoughts running through my head. Could I keep it up? Would the goals keep coming? Would the team keep winning? What if I got hurt? If I got hurt, I was screwed. And why couldn't Maria Solana have come a year earlier, when I was a junior? *[laughs]*

It was such an exciting time. Very tense, too, I guess, since there was so much uncertainty, but still... exciting. No scholarship offers *yet*, but at least they'd noticed me. At least they were interested.

Susan Douglas, right winger: I don't know when it was. We were maybe 9-0. 10-0. It was around then that my living situation got better.

I'd been going foster home to foster home for a while. Maybe two, two and a half months. Keeping it all secret, of course. Not telling a soul.

[pauses]

That's no way to go through life, you know? I was just a shell of a girl back then. Hardly said a word to anyone, scared they'd see how messed up I was. That's no way to live.

[pauses]

Well, anyway, the team was cooking along, 9-0, 10-0, something like that, and that was when I moved in with the Galtons. They were this nice old couple. Had never taken in a foster kid before. I was their first one. Mr. Galton was a retired college professor, Mrs. Galton a retired nurse. Nice house, nice people, everything about it was just nice. And since I was the first kid they'd ever taken in, they were kind of open to how it should be done. They didn't have any preconceptions, you know? So I came in and they treated me really well. Not like just another broken-down foster kid, but like a regular person. A normal kid.

That really makes a difference, you know? Some foster families, they get so many kids, one after the other after the other, that they hardly seem like kids to them any more. But with the Galtons, I was it. I was their first kid. Their only kid. So it was like their granddaughter had come to visit or something. Sitting around the table for dinner, going out for ice cream, taking me to see movies. Stuff like that.

I felt special. And it had been a long time since I'd felt special.

Nykesha Nolan, head coach: I'm super-competitive, so of course I wanted to know where we ranked. But with high school sports, state rankings are hard to come by. It's not like college football where, you know, the Associated Press has a top 25 and ESPN's got a top 25. This is high school. And even worse, it's high school *soccer*. And even worse, it's high school *girls* soccer. So try finding anybody who's paying attention. Much less paying attention enough to rank all the teams in the state. You'll have a hard time finding that guy.

But it turns out, there was a guy doing just that. Some guy on the internet who, for whatever reason, was a soccer freak and decided that high school soccer was gonna be his thing. So he had this website and each week he'd put out a top 10 for both boys and girls in our state.

Start of the year, of course, we were nowhere to be found. And why would we be? We were nobodies.

East Sycamore, they were number one. Right from the start. That program was so good, year in and year out, of course they were number one. Even in an off year, I bet they were in the top 10, just because Carlos Orostieta was their coach. But that year... that year was definitely *not* an off year. They were loaded. Number one, right from the start.

But did we eventually make the top 10? You bet we did. After four or five games, I think. We were undefeated, just killing teams, and then, one week there we were, in the top ten.

Win a few more, and we've climbed into the top 5. Win a few more, and we've made it to the top 3. I'm going crazy, the girls are going crazy, it was just so much fun.

I'm not sure when it was... I think we were 10-0. Maybe 11-0. And who was coming across town? To play us on *our field*? The top ranked, undefeated, completely loaded, completely unbeatable East Sycamore High School.

Oh, man alive, were we excited. We couldn't wait.

Destinee Jones, left winger, team captain: Seriously, we were so pumped for that game. Finally, we had a chance to beat those dudes. Finally, we were on their level!

AT least, we *thought* we were on their level. Were we? Who knows? But we couldn't wait to find out.

The whole school was excited. Okay, maybe not the whole school, but still, more people than usual. My family was even excited, believe it or not. Dad was like, "Number 3 in the state? Really... I may need to come see what this is all about." That's how he talks.

11v11

The football team had a bye that week, so my brothers were gonna come, too.

So I was like, damn, not only are we up against the best team in the state, but my family's finally gonna come see me play? We've gotta win this. If Dad comes to see me and we *lose*? He'd never come back. Never. We've *got* to win this game.

East Sycamore High School

Carlos Orostieta, head coach: As the first game approached, I had to make a decision on who would be my captain. I considered giving the armband to Hayley Swanson, you know. Just to avoid the trouble. But that would have been a cowardly move. It had to be Kaitlyn or Catalina.

When Friday came and the team was getting ready for our first game, I made the decision. I gave the armband to Kaitlyn.

It was the right decision. Yes, Hayley Swanson may have been our best player, and, yes, Catalina and Lisa and the rest of the defense, they were the *strength* of the team, but let me tell you, the *heart* of the team? The heart? Why, that was Kaitlyn Baker. So much passion.

So much intensity. She led that team, without a doubt. The captain's armband belonged to her.

I can tell you, my friend, that decision did not go over well with Catalina Forero. The rest of the team was okay with it, but Catalina, no.

Catalina Forero, center back: God, I was pissed. Just *pissed.* All the time I'd put into that team? All the years? And then Kaitlyn shows up out of nowhere and is captain? Yeah, it sucked. I was bitter.

The first game of the year – I don't remember who it was against. Somebody. It doesn't matter – I kind of had a black cloud following me around the field that day. I don't think it hurt my play, not that I remember – we shut them out. We had a lot of shutouts that year – but it hurt my enjoyment of the game, that's for sure. Kaitlyn was up there in center midfield and, you know, doing all her typical Kaitlyn stuff, running her mouth the whole time. *Watch this girl! Watch that girl! Keep it tight! Dump it off! Swing it!* Just non-stop, the whole game. And I was on the back line, just resenting the hell out of her.

I think it was the 70th minute, maybe the 75th when she got hurt. Right near the end. *[pauses]* Wait, you know high school games only go 80 minutes, right? Okay, good. Not everybody knows that.

So anyway, it's late in the game and Kaitlyn's hurt. Not hurt bad, just got knocked in the leg or something. Kaitlyn played hard as hell – still does – so she picked up knocks now and then. So in maybe like the 75th minute, she took a knee to her hip or something like that. Deep bruise, lot of pain. We were up 1-0, maybe 2-0. I'm not sure the other team even had a shot. It was an easy win. So Coach decides Kaitlyn's done for the day. Welp, as she's limping off the field, she comes over to me with the armband. She was like, "Here you go, Catalina. Take us the rest of the way."

And I refused. Turned and walked away. I think she ended up giving it to Hayley.

Kaitlyn Baker, central midfielder, team captain: Yeah, that was a mess. That was a bad situation.

I don't think I realized how angry Catalina was until then. I knew she wanted to be captain – who wouldn't? – but I didn't realize she was holding as much anger as that.

I think... That whole thing, I think it was a little bit of an eye-opener for me. In a way, it's actually a good thing Catalina refused the armband that first game. Because it kind of made me stop and think, *Wait, hold on, maybe this is more complicated than I'd thought. Maybe there's more to being captain than just motivating people, egging them on, being the hardest worker, leading by example. Maybe a captain's also got to make sure everyone feels like they're a part of the team.*

Because I think that's part of what was happening with Catalina. If she's not captain, is she still a part of the team? I had to convince her she was.

Catalina Forero, center back: Looking back on it from ten years later, it all seems stupid, but at the time, it really got in my head. That's what it's like when you're young, I think. You're dealing with stuff for the first time and you don't always handle it well. The thing with Kaitlyn? Not being named captain? I didn't handle it well. Refusing the armband that first game? I couldn't have handled that any worse. That was so stupid of me. So childish. But again, like I said, I was a kid. We were all kids. We were dealing with stuff for the first time, and sometimes you make mistakes.

Kaitlyn and I, we worked it out. Not all in one fell swoop, of course. It took a while. There were some fights. Some resentment. But we figured it out. Eventually.

And if she ever had to leave a game? I never refused the armband again.

Lisa Roney, center back: The Kaitlyn/Catalina thing? I tried really hard not to get caught up in that. I mean, being part of the back line, playing next to Catalina every day, how could I not? And sure, I guess I was on her side. But in a lot of ways, I just wanted it to settle down so we could play soccer.

The team was doing great. Just fabulous. How many wins did we have to start the season? A bunch. And they were all, like, 1-0, 2-0, that sort of thing. The offense? Nothing special. But the defense? Man, we were rock solid. Friggin' Hayley Swanson in goal, me and Catalina in front of her. Estefania and Sylvia *[Danielson]* out to the sides. That's a hell of a defense. That's a rock-solid defense. Opposing teams, they'd sometimes get lucky. Score on a penalty kick or something. But other than that? Nothing. Hell, sometimes they wouldn't even get a shot off. It was fabulous.

Our offense? It was only so-so. But that was fine, because if they gave us even a single goal, the game was won. That's how confident we were.

And you know how it is, when your team's winning, that eases a lot of tension. The Kaitlyn/Catalina thing? It settled down. Winning will do that.

Estefania Higuain, left back: I told you how hard that year was, but in some ways, I felt really, really lucky, you know? My family, we didn't move so I could be on this great team. We moved for Hugo. For the hospital. But it just so happened that the nearest high school had the best soccer team in the state. And I'm their starting left back? How lucky is that?

Hugo loved it, of course. "Tell me about the game. Who scored the goal?" And of *course* he wanted to hear about Kaitlyn Baker. He loved her. Never laid an eye on her, but he loved her. "Did she get another yellow card? Did she yell at the ref again? Is she still fighting with Catalina?"

Like I told you, sometimes, even if nothing happened,

I'd make up stuff to tell Hugo. Just to see him light up. He needed something good in his life.

[long pause]

I'm sorry. It's still hard to talk about.

[long pause]

Hugo was dying. It was clear. The team was winning, I was playing well, but at home, my brother was dying. Actually, he wasn't always at home. At a certain point, he had to move into the hospital full-time. The thing they were doing – chemo, I guess. I'm not sure – it wasn't working anymore, and they wanted to try something new.

That was such a hard time. For him, for me, for the whole family. Hugo was a skeleton. Sick all the time. And now, living in the hospital.

I could walk there from school. The hospital was actually closer to school than to home, so I would usually have soccer practice, then go straight to the hospital. Hugo, he was bad, he was tired, but he still wanted to hear all the details. I'm glad we were a good team. I'm glad I could tell him about wins, not losses. Maybe it helped a little, there at the end.

Chamique Lennox, backup goalkeeper: Yeah, we were great. I think the team started 9-0, 10-0, maybe more. I can't remember.

You know, I say "*We* were great," but I was barely part of the team at that point. Hayley was dominant. Even way back then, she was crazy-good. And with her playing every minute, the team hardly needed a backup keeper, much less two. In practice, Hayley was doing most of the drills. Ruthann would do a few, then I'd do a *very* few. Mostly I watched. I guess you can learn a lot watching a badass like Hayley. I don't know. I just know I didn't really have much to do with those first however many games we won at the start of the year.

I got to go on the bus, though. You know, for away games. It was so great. Lisa and I would sit together and hold hands and kind of cuddle a little bit. Not cuddle, exactly, but you know, just kind of lean up against each other and stuff. Maybe little tiny kisses. The other girls, they teased us some. *Lisa and Chamique... sittin' in a tree... K-I-S-S-I-N-G.* You know, stupid stuff. I loved that, too. I loved how Lisa would just lean over and kiss me while flipping everyone the bird. *[laughs]* She didn't care. I loved that confidence. I didn't have it, of course, but I loved how she did.

Gosh, there's nothing like your first girlfriend, you know? It's just so exciting. So scary, so exciting. Kissing for the first time, God how great was that? I'd actually kissed a boy before, at a party back in middle school. Spin the bottle. But, oh man, kissing a girl is... there's no comparison. None. And, you know, holding hands, too. Just something simple like that, it was so wonderful, doing it all for the first time.

11v11

Lisa Roney, center back: It was fun watching Chamique deal with coming out. I'd had to do it myself just a couple years earlier. We all go through it. Every gay person in the world. It's different for everyone, I guess. But also the same.

Chamique handled it really well. Came out to herself, came out to me, came out to a few of my gay friends. A lot of girls would've stopped there, but no, Chamique was all-in. She was like, *Let's do this. Let's be gay.* So then she was coming out to the team, coming out to the school. She did all this in, like, a month. Maybe two months, tops. So brave. So enthusiastic.

Dating someone who's going through all those changes, all those big milestones, it's fun. It's exciting. It's almost like you're going through them as well.

I really enjoyed that time with Chamique. I know she was just a freshman, but I really liked her. She was a hell of a girl.

Chamique Lennox, backup goalkeeper: The last step was coming out to my family, and that was *terrifying*. I'm not even sure why, because my parents are super-cool. I shouldn't have been so afraid, but I was.

But still, I knew I had to do it. I had to come out to them. Because I was going through this amazing, wonderful, life-changing thing, you know? And I wanted my family in on it. I wanted them to be a part of it. I wanted to be able to talk to Mom about Lisa – tell her about dates, ask her for advice, all that stuff, all that normal teenager dating stuff – and I couldn't. It was awful.

So, eventually, I was like, *I don't care if it's scary. I've got to do this. I've got to be brave.*

Lisa Roney, center back: I was there, but I didn't know it was gonna happen. Chamique just sort of surprised me with it.

It was before a game, I can't remember which one. Maybe a month or two into the season? It was a home game and the whole team's walking from the locker room out to the field. Uniforms on, cleats clickity-clacking on the sidewalk, Chamique and I walking together. All of a sudden, she says something like, "Oh, it's my mom and dad. What are they doing here?" She starts waving and points to this couple up ahead and I'm like, *Oh, cool*, you know, not really thinking much. Then she grabs my arm and starts pulling me toward them. "Let's go say hi."

I knew she wasn't out with her parents, so I was immediately on guard. I was like, *Okay, how do I play this?* You know, I didn't want to stand too close to Chamique, didn't want them to think we were more than friends, didn't want to do anything to give Chamique away.

But then she was like, "Hey, Mom. Hey, Dad." Kissed them on the cheek, probably. And then, "This is my girlfriend, Lisa."

I was immediately like, *Wait, what?* Her parents were, too. They've got this confused look on their faces, I've got this confused look on *my* face, and Chamique's there in the middle of us, slipping her arm around my waist. "We've been dating for a while now."

[laughs]

Man, the guts that girl had. So brave.

Chamique Lennox, backup goalkeeper: I wasn't brave. I was terrified. But you know that thing they say, *Fake it 'til you make it?* That's completely true. In almost everything.

I had to fake it a lot that year. I was this little freshman girl, this little baby lesbian, all scared and stuff, but I didn't want to be. I wanted to be brave. So I faked it. I faked being brave. And it worked. Completely and totally.

Fake it 'til you make it, man. It works.

Carlos Orostieta, head coach: 10-0, I think we started. Or was it 11-0? No, it was 12-0! Or was it? *[laughs]* My old brain, I can barely remember. I know we were very, very good.

The defense was the key, of course. It was very, very strong. Our games, they were usually 1-0. 2-0. I don't know how many goals Hayley Swanson gave up that year, but it was not many. Maybe a penalty kick here, a deflected shot there, but otherwise, nothing. An amazing keeper, Hayley was. Still is, of course. Did you see her in the last World Cup? The Japan game? Oh, my goodness! How many saves did she make that day? Amazing!

But anyway, the season was going well. Giving Kaitlyn Baker the captain's armband, that turned out to be the right decision. The whole season, she was the one who pushed the team. When things got tough, was I the one yelling and screaming? No, I was an old man. *[laughs]* After 40 seasons, I didn't have a lot of screaming and yelling left in me. Kaitlyn, though, she still had that fire. If it was late in a game and people were moving a little slow, Kaitlyn would let them hear about it. When she saw someone she thought could be working harder, she let them hear about it.

Most of the time, she did it well. Most of the time she knew when to yell and when to stop. But there were some missteps. Of course there were. She was young, and her passion, it could get the best of her. Maybe she would get on a teammate a bit too much and there would be bruised feelings.

And, yes, there were some ejections, too. There were some red cards. *[laughs]* Kaitlyn would feel a teammate had been hard done by, and perhaps she would tell the referee a little too strongly. Use some language. Get herself ejected. *[laughs]* I think she missed one or two games that way.

Did it frustrate me a little? Sure. But it was a price I was willing to pay. The team needed Kaitlyn's passion.

They needed her heart.

But of course, in the end, that season wasn't about Kaitlyn Baker. It was about the defense. Hayley Swanson. Roney and Forero. Higuain and Danielson. My goodness, what a defense!

Kaitlyn Baker, central midfielder, team captain: Nobody put up major stats. I scored a couple goals. Maybe three, tops. *[Forward Gloria]* Cayetano and *[midfielder Vilma]* Aguilar, they might've had three or four each. Scoring was a group effort. A goal here, a goal there, that's how we did it.

But the defense? Who needed goals with a defense like that? As far as teamwork goes, I'm not sure I've played with a better back four. Even to this day. I mean that. Those four girls, plus Hayley Swanson behind them, they were like a well-oiled machine. How many goals did they give up that year? Three? Four? I'm not even sure it was that much.

Three national team players. Two World Cup starters. That's who I had playing behind me. In high school! It's insane.

Catalina Forero, center back: We were 11-0 when we played West. They were, too, which was crazy. West Sycamore? Good? They were never good. I mean, ask us who our rival was and we wouldn't say West Sycamore. We'd say North Sycamore. Maybe Ravenscroft. Or Jefferson. But West? They were just this school across town. I think football was their thing.

Maybe basketball. Certainly not soccer. And here they were, 11-0 and ranked number three in the state. Crazy.

So yeah, we were excited. The season was going well, we were cruising along, and now we were gonna get to see what this crazy West Sycamore team was all about.

We talked, of course. "Oh, did you hear? West beat so-and-so 5-0." "Oh, did you hear? Maria Solana got player of the week again." That sort of thing. Their team, it's kinda like they were a myth or something. Were they real? No one knew. Was their offense as good as it seemed? Did Maria Solana walk on water? *[laughs]*

So everyone was really excited. We were finally gonna get to play them, finally see if they were the real deal. 11-0 versus 11-0. I was so pumped.

Estefania Higuain, left back: That whole day was very exciting. I remember it well. The game was at their place, so we had to bus across town. It was my first time going to West Sycamore, of course. Everyone told me they usually weren't too good, but that year? My goodness, everyone was talking about them. Hugo even knew about them. "You've got to tell me about this Solana girl," he said. She was scoring like two or three goals a game, you know. Like Lionel Messi or something. Everyone wanted to see her. Hugo, me, the whole team.

So we ride the bus across town and we file off and we're on their field doing our warm ups. Kaitlyn's leading us, of course. Stretches, warm up drills, all the usual. But we're all kind of distracted, we're all sort of halfway watching West warm up over on their half of the field. We're checking them out, trying to see who's who. Sylvia and I were next to each other and she was like, "Which one's Solana? None of them look like anything special. Is that her? Number 17? Is that her?"

Well, finally it's game time and Coach pulls the whole team together and tells us Solana's not there. She's got a cold or something. Home in bed, eating chicken soup and sneezing.

Oh, it was *so* disappointing!

Carlos Orostieta, head coach: In the end, it was a normal game for us. 1-0 we won. I think West got two or three shots on goal, which I have to tell you, is more than most teams got against us that year. So clearly there was still talent on that team. But without Solana? No, they could not break us down.

I felt bad for Nykesha Nolan. She was a good young coach. Very energetic, very exciting. I liked her a great deal. When we talked before the game, I could see how upset she was. And then after the game, she told me she'd been looking at the game as a real test. A test to see how good their team really was.

If they'd had Solana that day, would they have won? I cannot say. I think they would have gotten more shots. Maybe put a real scare in us. But remember, we had some pretty good players, too. *[laughs]* So there is no telling.

After the game, Nykesha and I, we shook hands. "Maybe we'll meet in the playoffs," I told her. "And then, we'll both be full strength, okay?"

Oh, my. If only I could have seen into the future.

Chamique Lennox, backup goalkeeper: Ruthann was sick that next week. Tuesday at practice, Wednesday at practice, Thursday at practice, she was home sick, so, you know, my life suddenly got a whole lot busier. I'm playing in the opposite net during scrimmages, helping Hayley with her drills, all the stuff Ruthann normally did. Second-string keeper stuff.

Then Friday comes around and we've got our game that day and Ruthann's *still* not there. Coach comes and finds me and says, "Good news, kid. You've been promoted."

Turns out, it wasn't just a cold Ruthann had. She had *mono*. She was gonna be sick for *weeks*. Maybe the rest of the season. So Coach is being super-serious with me. I mean, he's still sweet and kind and funny, because, you know, he's Coach, but still, he's like, "You need to be ready to play, Chamique. Physically ready, mentally ready, emotionally ready. You're Hayley's backup now. The team's counting on you."

I was terrified. I pretended I wasn't, but I was. Just terrified.

11v11

Kaitlyn Baker, central midfielder, team captain: Beating West had put us at 12-0. We were ranked first in the state, we had two games left in the regular season, everything was going pretty much perfectly. Honestly, I figured we'd enter the playoffs 14-0, then roll to the title. I was totally confident.

And, of course, what happens? It all falls apart.

The game was on the road. Who was it against? I want to say Clifford Hills. They were nothing special. Just your average team. Nothing to worry about.

First half, we scored on a corner. I'm almost positive it was Roney. One of those typical ugly goals we scored a lot of that year. Ye-Jee *[Park, the team's right midfielder]* lofts the corner kick into the middle of the box and Roney out-jumps someone. 1-0, just like that.

With our team that year, as soon as we got a goal, we felt we'd won the game. Seriously. Our defense was that good. Take that game for example, Clifford Hills didn't get a single shot in the first half. And I'm not talking shots on *goal*, I'm talking shots, period. They didn't have a single shot. They could barely get the ball across midfield. Our back four was playing a super-high line, the midfield, we were pressuring the hell out of the ball, shutting things down before they started, and Hayley Swanson was back there in goal, bored out of her mind, I'm sure. Doing her Math homework, probably. That's how a lot of our games were that year.

So, as I recall, it was right after halftime that it happened. Clifford Hills, they were really pushing, really trying to move forward, and one of their girls, she finally gets the ball across midfield, and she probably thinks to herself, *Well, I should just go ahead and shoot from here. Because, you know, we may never get this close again.* So she fires this super-long shot. It was from, I don't know, forty yards out. Not a terribly dangerous shot. Fairly soft. But it loops over the back line, bounces, and is heading for goal. Not dangerous or anything. Not moving fast. But at least it was on target, right? At least Swanson has to put away her homework and save the thing, right? *[laughs]*

So what happens? Swanson goes down on one knee, scoops it up, and what does she do? Breaks her finger. Can you believe it? Jams a finger into the ground and breaks it. Unbelievable.

We didn't realize it right away. Not even Swanson. She knew it hurt... but broken? No. She stayed in the game for a few minutes, but then the finger started swelling and the pain got to be too much and she had to go out. You should've seen her finger when she pulled off her gloves. Swollen up like a sausage. I was standing there with her and Coach and a few others. Soon as I saw it, I knew she was done for the day.

And on such a simple play, too. Such a nothing play. I mean, if your goalkeeper's going to break her finger, it should be on some spectacular diving play, right? Not kneeling down and scooping up some soft little rolling ball.

But, anyway, that was it for Swanson. And since our backup keeper had mono, who's coming in? Our backup's backup. Chamique Lennox.

Chamique Lennox, backup goalkeeper: It was like my worst nightmare. I can't even describe how scared I was.

I'd been the backup for, what, three days? Not even three days, since all that time at practice, I'd just assumed Ruthann would be back the next day. So, really, I'd only *truly* been the backup for, what, two hours?

So there I was, sitting on the bench, and Coach turns and yells over to me, "Chamique. Get your gloves on. You're going in."

I still remember the way my stomach dropped. I turned to the girl next to me – I don't remember who it was. Another bench warmer – and I was like, "What did he say?" I'm not even sure I said that much. I was probably just silent, my mouth open or something.

I know I was silent when I was walking onto the field. I got off the bench and was walking onto the field and Coach was like, "Your gloves! Get your gloves!" And I looked down and realized I didn't have them on, so I ran back to the bench and got them. And then I couldn't put them on right. Maybe I was putting them on the wrong hands or something. *[laughs]* It's funny *now*, looking back, but at the time, it was awful. It's like I was in a trance or something.

So I finally got the gloves on and was walking onto the field and Coach probably said something, but I don't know what. I was pretty much deaf. That walk out to the goal was in super slow motion. It just took forever. Players were saying things to me. Who knows what. I didn't hear any of it. All I heard was my pulse in my ears. All I felt was my stomach dragging along on the ground, getting caught up in my feet.

Eventually, there I was in goal. Hopefully facing the right direction. *[laughs]* I don't know what I looked like to everyone else. Maybe I looked like a real goalkeeper. Like I knew what I was doing. But honestly, in my head, there was nothing. My mind was a complete blank. Deer in the headlights.

Lisa Roney, center back: It was awful. I felt so bad for her. I wanted to just wrap my arms around her and hold her but, you know, you can't do that on a soccer field. And anyway, we had a game to play. The ref blew the whistle and suddenly we were live again. Or, barely alive. It was crazy how losing Hayley took the air out of everyone.

I want to be completely clear on this; Chamique did not lose us that game. The entire team is to blame. The entire team fell apart. I mean, come on, we gave up three goals in the second half. Three goals! We go from giving up one lame shot from midfield in the entire game to giving up three goals in thirty minutes? That's not the keeper's fault. That's the whole defense falling apart. Me, Catalina, the fullbacks, the midfield, everyone. We were a mess. Completely shaken.

And the thing is, we knew it. I've gotta give the team credit. No one was blaming Chamique. Well, not really. A couple times, Catalina yelled at her, "You've gotta talk to us! You've gotta tell us what you're doing back there!"

I was like, "Cut her some slack, Cat! She's out of her league!"

To be honest, I'm not sure that was the right thing to say. I mean, one, I was in a weird spot, considering Chamique was my girlfriend and all. And also, Chamique heard that. She heard me talking about how lost she was. Which couldn't have been good for her confidence.

Well, what are you going to do? It was the truth. Chamique was overwhelmed. We couldn't count on her to help us stay organized. The rest of us needed to step up and do it without her. And clearly, we failed.

Jeesh. How does a defense fall apart that completely? Three goals. Three. That probably matched our season total up to that point. It was awful. We're all to blame.

After the game, Chamique was just devastated. We all were, but she was the worst. We sat together on the bus ride home, but there wasn't much to say. It was a pretty quiet bus. Our perfect season was gone, our all-star goalie was done, and we'd just shown that we couldn't win without her.

That bus ride home was probably the low point of the whole season.

Estefania Higuain, left back: Wow, things got so bad those last couple weeks. Everything. The team, my family, everything was just awful.

We had our first loss on Friday, and then that weekend, Hugo's health fell apart. Just a serious, serious downturn. We'd had him at home for a week or two, but that weekend he had to go back to the hospital.

And then Monday we find out Hayley's done for the year. It wasn't a broken finger, it was a torn ligament, but that didn't really matter. Her season was over. Our best player, gone.

And, of course, that meant the playoffs were no longer a sure thing. Only eight teams in the whole state made the playoffs, you know. Some years, 12-2 would get you in. Some years, it wouldn't. We'd started 12-0, which helped, but now we were 12-1. If we lost our last game, would we make it in?

We'd gone from being a sure thing to having our backs completely against the wall.

Carlos Orostieta, head coach: Oh, yes, my friend, it was difficult. It was very, very difficult.

I had to find a backup goalkeeper, of course. How do

you like that? I go from having three to having one. And the one I have is this poor freshman who wasn't even planning on going out for the team!

I think what I ended up doing was... I went to somebody. The basketball coach, I think. Their season hadn't started yet, so I asked her, "Who's your best athlete?" Whoever the girl was, I told her, "Congratulations, you're our new backup goalkeeper. See you at practice this afternoon." *[laughs]* Can you believe it?

So, obviously, that was a busy week of practice. You would think most of my time would be spent coaching Chamique, but to be honest, Hayley Swanson did most of that. Her hand was in a splint, I think, but there she was anyway, working with Chamique. Running her through drills, working on her fundamentals. Her shot-stopping. Her distribution. Hayley was wonderful, to be honest. A natural coach. Mark my words, Hayley Swanson will be coaching someday. When her playing career ends – whenever that is – she will be coaching somewhere. I am sure of it.

So that freed me to work with the rest of the team. Get them ready to play without Hayley. Not an easy task, I can tell you. As good as that back four was? You'd be surprised how much they relied on Hayley behind them. For communication, you see. Hayley was always very vocal. Always telling her defense where she was, what she saw, what she needed them to do.

Could Chamique do all that? Goodness, no. Not a

chance. She was tall and quick and could stop shots well, but she was still learning the game. And she was behind two incredibly good, very experienced center backs. Asking a freshman to yell at Catalina Forero? At Lisa Roney? That was a lot to ask.

Friday's game – the season's final game – was against Jefferson. We lost 2-1.

On the whole, our defense was better than it had been against Clifford Hills. Chamique was silent in goal, of course, but Catalina and Lisa covered for her. They did the yelling. Both for Chamique and *at* Chamique. Lisa, especially. Just letting Chamique know where to be, you know. What to watch for.

So yes, I would call it a better performance by the defense. Two goals conceded over 80 minutes versus three goals conceded over 30? That's an improvement, I would say. But still, a loss is a loss. Two straight losses and we ended the regular season 12-2.

Catalina Forero, center back: The game was at home, so as soon as it was over, as soon as we'd lost, we were all back in the locker room checking our phones, finding out how other teams were doing. It was a mess. There were a bunch of teams hovering around that 13-1, 12-2, 11-3 area. If we were gonna make the playoffs, we needed a few teams to lose. We needed a little help.

Long story short, we got in. Barely. I think we were the eighth and final seed. Actually, I know we were, because our first round game was against the top seed, Wade Central, who were 14-0.

They were cruising along, we were a mess. They were full strength, we were playing our third-string keeper. It's not how anyone imagined us entering the playoffs.

West Sycamore High School

Nykesha Nolan, head coach: So we finished the year 13-1 and ranked second. Hell of a record, a lot better than anyone expected, but still... damn that loss to East. We should've been undefeated. Ten years later and it still annoys me. Which is dumb.

But the truth is, the way that one loss happened, with Maria being sick, that's a loss we could live with. Everyone knew we'd have beaten East full strength. Heck, down our best player and we still played 'em close? That's nothing to be ashamed of. And we knew it. Full strength, we knew we could beat anyone.

So here comes the tournament, we're the second seed, we'll be playing the seventh seed, South Hawthorne, and we're playing them at home. It was an exciting week of practice. Lots of confidence, lots of smiles. It felt like everything was set up for us to roll through the playoffs.

Destinee Jones, left winger, team captain: I wanted revenge for that East Sycamore loss. First game my dad had ever come to see and we can't even score a goal. He was all like, "Oh, a 1-0 game. Soccer's so exciting. Yawn." And I was trying to tell him that if Maria had been healthy, we might've dropped 5 goals on them. But nope, we get shut out. It was humiliating. Mom was like, "No, I've seen them score. They're exciting, really." My dad, my friggin' brothers... they were unimpressed.

But the way the tournament was seeded – us the 2nd seed, East the 8th – if we wanted revenge, it was gonna have to be in the final. East would have to beat the top seed, then I guess the fourth or fifth seed, and only then would we get to play them. And this time, it would be them who was down their best player, not us. We'd be full strength, they'd be missing Hayley Swanson, and we'd get to pay them back for that one loss.

And maybe, *maybe*, I could get my family out there to watch it. I mean, hell, if we could make it to the final, they'd have to come watch, right?

Susan Douglas, right winger: Yeah, I was really looking forward to the playoffs. It was hard not to be excited.

That was a pretty good time for me. Life was decent.

For the first time in months, really. I was still with the Galtons. I liked them, they liked me. It looked like a situation that could last, you know? I was thinking, *Wow, what if I could just stay here? No more moving to a new home every couple weeks. Just stay in one spot for awhile.* Getting excited about something like that won't make sense to most people, but all the foster kids out there, they'll understand. When you find a good situation, you're praying you don't have to give it up.

So, yeah, going into the playoffs, I was actually feeling good. Best I had in months. Of course, I was still living a lie, still keeping my situation a secret from everyone. That hadn't changed. But on the inside? Things were good. I was looking forward to the playoffs. Excited to see how we'd do.

Clementine Thiamale, central defensive midfielder: It was a good week of practice. We were all very confident. I think Destinee Jones was a big part of that. She was so excited, so full of energy. Destinee was a good captain. I've had a lot of captains over the years and she was one of the best. Some captains are too serious, too competitive. Some captains are too quiet and will never speak up for you. Destinee was a good combination of things. Maria Solana was the best player on that team, but Destinee deserves a lot of credit, too.

So, yes, that week was good. We felt like we had a really good chance to win it all.

11v11

I remember... *[laughs]* Okay, this is embarrassing, but I think that was the week Curtis finally asked me out. Was it? I think it was.

He'd been coming around a lot. You know, to flirt and stuff. He would stop by my locker between classes. He would call me at home to ask about homework. My dad, he didn't like that. *[laughs]* And that week leading up to the tournament, I think Curtis came to a couple practices. Yes, I'm sure of it now, because I remember this one day we were practicing and it was very cold. One of the first really cold days of the year. We were on the practice field, Coach was talking to us about South Hawthorne, the team we'd be playing, and I remember Curtis was sitting on the bleachers, all hunched up in this big coat, with these huge clouds of breath around him. Some of the girls were teasing me, telling me, "Oh, your boyfriend's here." And I was like, "He's not my boyfriend," and then Destinee came right up beside me and grabbed my hand and made me wave at him and she yelled, "Hi, Curtis!" *[laughs]* I was so embarrassed, but Curtis just smiled and waved.

Gosh, that's a pretty silly story, but... I don't know, when you're that age and you've never had a boyfriend before, small things like that are very exciting.

Anyway, after practice, I went over to him and told him I couldn't believe he sat through all that cold and he was just so sweet and so cute and said he wanted to see me play and then we walked back to the school together and he asked me out.

I don't think you ever forget your first time doing things, you know? Maybe some girls get asked out all the time, but that was a first for me, so I think it will always be special.

So that week wasn't all about soccer, I guess. There was life, too.

Martha Sullivan, forward: That week was all about soccer. Life, boys, family, I didn't want to think about any of that. I was totally focused on soccer. Soccer and college. How I could use soccer to get myself to college.

Colorado State was the school that seemed most interested in me, but Georgia Tech was where I wanted to go. I was thinking I might like computer programming and Tech seemed like a good school for that. Plus, I thought it would be cool to live in a big city like Atlanta.

I'd talked to Tech's coach on the phone and she liked my numbers, liked all my goals. She said something like, "Let's wait until after the playoffs to make a decision. You keep playing hard, do well, and we'll be in touch." So that lit a fire under me. I was like, *I've got to do well. The team's got to win, I've got to score, and then she'll offer me a scholarship.*

So yeah, you could say I was motivated. All soccer, all the time. South Hawthorne, they didn't stand a chance.

Maria Solana, central attacking midfielder: The

game was Friday. My family came. My parents, my sisters. Everyone was very excited. It was cold, as I remember it. Cold, but dry.

The game started well. I scored the first goal, I think it was in the fifth minute. I can't remember it perfectly, but I think it was from outside the box. A longer shot. Yes, I think it went into the top corner.

It was good to get that goal so early. It's always good to get an early goal. That year, teams were frightened of our offense, so they would sit back, keep their defense very, very tight. Make it very hard for us to do anything.

But when you get an early goal, it helps. Then the other team, they have to come out and play. They can't sit back. They have to move forward. Which means there's more chance for you to score a second goal.

Martha Sullivan, forward: Our second goal was in the 20th minute, I think. Somewhere around then. Maria set it up, big surprise. She and Daniela were right on the edge of the box, doing a little back-and-forth thing. You know, small little passes. The defense was totally focused on that, wondering how Maria was going to beat them.

Meanwhile, I'm in their blind spot, totally invisible. I make a quick little run to the back post, Maria slips a pass between a couple girls, and suddenly – *Oh, wait, where did she come from?* – I'm tapping it into goal.

Goodness me, how many goals did I score just like that? Maria Solana was a gift from heaven. Maria Solana got me my scholarship, plain and simple.

Destinee Jones, left winger, team captain: So, it's like the 30th minute and we're up 2-0, and South Hawthorne's getting desperate. They're all like, *Oh, dude, we gotta pick it up. We've gotta push forward, push forward, push forward, or else, you know, our season's over.* That's what they're thinking.

But what we're thinking is, *Yeah, fine, push forward all you want. That just means your defense'll be all stretched out and we're gonna punish you.*

And that's what happened on the third goal. They're pushing forward, desperate. One of our girls gets the ball – Clementine, probably – she makes the quick outlet pass to Maria, and just like that, we're charging down the field on a counter. Susan and Maria are over on the right side, pass, pass, pass, then Maria's firing it into the back of the net. Boom, 3-0.

Everyone's happy, all's right in the world, and nothing could possibly go wrong, right?

Wrong.

Nykesha Nolan, head coach: Oh, dear sweet baby Jesus, how wrong it went. How wrong it went.

Ask yourself, *What's the worst possible thing that could happen to this team?*

Yep, that's what happened.

It was maybe the 38th minute? 39th? Right before the half. Remember, high school soccer has 40 minute halves, not 45 like everywhere else. So it was right about then. Just before half. We were up 3-0. Two goals for Solana, another for Sullivan. Everything's going according to plan.

And then it happens.

Destinee Jones, left winger, team captain: I remember it like it was yesterday. Awful play. Scary as hell.

It was another counter-attack. A really fast counter, right up the center of the field. I can't remember who started it, who laid the pass out there, but it was a nice leading pass Maria could run onto.

So there's the ball rolling along, Maria's running full speed after it, the South Hawthorne defender's coming full speed from the other direction, and sure enough, they get there at exactly the same time.

Was it a dirty play? I don't know. Not really. Just bad luck. The defender went in low, Maria went in high, and next thing you know, Maria's flying through the air. How far did she travel in the air? Five feet? Ten feet? 15? She did a full flip in the air, I know that. A full somersault, and I swear I'm not exaggerating. Ask anyone. She flipped head over heels, then *crashed* to the ground, like 10, 15 feet down the field. It was horrible. It was like something you'd see in a car race or something. Terrifying.

Well, no surprise, everything went silent. Everything. Both teams stopped, the people in the stands, the benches, the players on the field, everyone just went silent, eyes wide, holding their breath. I don't know about everyone else, but I was standing there thinking, *Is she even alive?*

Nykesha Nolan, head coach: Watching it from the sideline, it couldn't have looked worse. Maria actually *flipped.* Did you know that? She flipped, head over heels.

She didn't hit her head, so that's good. She landed kind of feet-first, but sideways, and really awkwardly, so her legs got all screwy under her. My immediate thought was, *It's her ACL. She just destroyed her knees.* I had a couple teammates who did that in college, just ripped their knees to bits, so that's the first place my mind went.

There was this pause of like, I don't know, five or 10 seconds, where everyone was silent, just kind of looking at her, then time kind of started up again, and everyone raced over to help her. I ran out onto the field, the ref was there, the whole team was there, all of us surrounding Maria on the ground.

She was looking a little dazed, to be honest. The pain didn't hit her right away. It's like that sometimes.

Maria Solana, central attacking midfielder: They say I did a flip, head over feet, but I don't remember it. I just remember being on the ground, and all these people were around me, and I wasn't sure how I got there.

It was my ankle that broke. My left ankle. I looked down at it, lying there on the ground, and it looked strange and was starting to hurt, and I knew something was very wrong. I'd never broken a bone, so I didn't know for sure, but the pain, it started to get very bad, and then it was swelling, and I was thinking, *Oh, it's broken, isn't it? This is very bad.*

Susan Douglas, right winger: Believe it or not, I didn't actually see the play because I was fixing my shoe. I know, right? Biggest play of the game – hell, biggest play of the *season* – and I didn't even see it. But the girl I was covering, she'd stepped on my heel and given me a flat tire, so I was down on one knee, fixing that. I heard everything go silent and I looked up and Maria was on the ground and everything had just stopped and I was like, *Uh oh, what did I miss?*

The game was stopped, obviously, so I ran over to see what was up. We were all standing around her. The players, the ref, Coach. Maria's face was all screwed up, just in agony. It was cold that day, too, which I'm sure didn't make it any better, lying there on the hard ground, freezing her tail off. A couple girls got her up, one under each arm, and took her off the field. I think she went straight to the hospital, didn't even stick around to see the rest of the game.

Which is probably for the best. The rest of the game was a disaster.

Nykesha Nolan, head coach: It was pretty much my worst nightmare, losing Solana. She *was* that team. Other than the game where she was sick, she'd played pretty much every minute of every game, all season long. She was the straw that stirred our drink. Now, here we were in the playoffs and I had to find another straw.

Destinee Jones, left winger, team captain: I mean, you literally could not pick a worse player for us to lose. Lose me? Fine. Lose Sullivan? Fine. Hell, even lose Clementine and we'd survive. But lose Maria? That was worst case scenario. That was sum of all fears. We were an offensive-minded team and she was our offense.

I tell ya, when they carried her off the field, the rest of us were looking at each other like, *Oh, damn. We're screwed. Scuh-rewed.* I mean, I was trying to be positive, trying to put on a good face. I didn't want the girls to get too down, but it wasn't easy. On the outside, I was like, "It's okay, we got this," but on the inside, I was like, *Oh, God, we're not okay. We ain't got this.*

Nykesha Nolan, head coach: Halftime was the worst. Solana was heading off to the hospital, the rest of the team's looking at me, hoping I've got some kind of plan, and I'm standing there with nothing. The East

Sycamore game, when Maria had been sick? I'd replaced her with Lindsey Cash and she'd been halfway decent. But now, Lindsey was on the bench, injured. I don't remember what is was. Foot. Groin. Doesn't matter. My best player's down and her backup's down, too.

You remember that first practice, way back in the preseason? How bad I blew that? How it made me question whether I could be a good coach? Well, this was a thousand times worse. Standing there, all those girls looking at me, expecting me to have some answer, some way to save things, that was rock bottom. That took the wind right out of me. I was just standing there, my stomach in a knot, thinking, *I've got nothing. I don't know anything about coaching. I was just riding the Maria Solana train. And now that train's broken down, so what the hell do I do now?*

But, I had to do something, right? So I told Deavon Pope to get in there for Solana. Which was a joke. Pope was a sophomore, just a kid. She'd played a few times on the wing, but just to give people a breather. A little at left winger, a little at right. She'd never played in the center because, well, no one had. But I had to throw someone in there, so I picked her.

She didn't want it, of course. Her eyes went wide – I remember it so clearly – her eyes went wide and she was shaking her head a little like, *No, Coach, I can't do that.* But what was I gonna do?

Destinee Jones, left winger, team captain: It was a

disaster. The offense couldn't do *anything*. Completely stagnated. The defense was no better. We gave up two goals in about 15 minutes. It was awful. I hadn't realized how much Maria helped our defense until Deavon came in there and just gave us nothing.

You know, it's easy to blame Deavon for all of this, but the truth is, she was put into a can't-win situation. She was just this little sophomore kid who never played and didn't think she *would* play. Now suddenly she's thrown into a game, in the playoffs, against a good team, and she's supposed to replace Maria Solana? You gotta feel for her.

Nykesha Nolan, head coach: That was a real eye-opener for me, watching Deavon stumbling around out there. It taught me that you can't rely on one player so much, even if that player's Maria Solana. It taught me to play my bench, to play my kids. Get 'em ready. Because you never know when your best player's gonna go down. You gotta be ready. That's what I learned that day.

But of course, those lessons didn't help me then. They've helped me since, but they didn't help me that day. That day all I could do was send this scared little backup winger out there and tell her to play central attacking midfielder. Tell her to run our offense. It was a mess.

Needless to say, we didn't score any more. The offense was dead in the water. All season long, we're an offensive juggernaut, and now we can hardly string two passes together. Spent pretty much the rest of the game back in our half, playing defense. Gave up two goals in, what, 10, 15 minutes? Could've given up three or four more. I think they hit the post a couple times. It was a nightmare.

Susan Douglas, right winger: At a certain point, Coach decided to flip me and Deavon. Put Deavon on the wing and give me a try in the middle.

Things got better. I didn't really improve the offense, but the defense tightened up a little. I guess I just had a better sense of what Maria did in the center of the field. Defensively, I mean. Offensively, nothing really changed.

Well, no, that's not true. We held a little possession, I guess. In fact, that's probably why the defense improved, too. In the center of the pitch, I could hold the ball a little. Dink it out to Destinee, get it back, dink it over to Deavon, get it back. Make little passes back to Clementine, back to the defense. I gotta be honest, those last – what was it, 20 minutes? – I was just playing keep-away. We still had the lead, and I figured, if we can hold the ball for the rest of the game, we can't give up another goal. So that's what I did. Dribbled around a lot. Made safe passes. Didn't try much going forward. Just played keep-away. Coach seemed okay with that. After giving up two goals in 15 minutes, she was just glad to stop the bleeding.

Nykesha Nolan, head coach: The only good thing that came out of that half was trying Susan Douglas in

Solana's spot. That improved things a bit. We could finally string a couple passes together. We could hold possession for a bit. It wasn't great, but it was at least better. It was something to build on for the next game.

We ended up winning 3-2. Damn miracle. And then it was on to the semis. I had a week to figure out how to play a full game without Maria Solana.

Maria Solana, central attacking midfielder: I was at the hospital until very late. So much waiting. I had an ice pack, but my ankle was still swollen and painful. Finally, they gave me the x-ray and saw it was broken, just like I'd thought. They put it into a boot and sent me home.

That was a terrible weekend for me. Not because of the pain or any of that, but because my heart was broken over the team. Yoreli came to the hospital after the game and told me everything. How we'd given up two goals, how everything had fallen apart. She was very sad. She didn't think we could win the next game without me. It was so awful to hear. These girls, they had become my friends, my second family. And now they were going to the semifinal, and I couldn't help them. It was heartbreaking.

So that weekend, at first I just wanted to be sad and miserable, but then I decided I had to stop that and think about the team. I had to find a way to help them, even with my broken ankle. Go to the practices. Go to the game. Help them get ready. I wasn't sure how, but somehow. I had to do something.

East Sycamore High School

Carlos Orostieta, head coach: The week before the playoffs, that was a difficult week. Very challenging. The girls, they were in a strange place mentally.

So much of coaching is psychological. Yes, there are tactics and training and all of those very important things, but psychology? Just as important. And perhaps harder to get right.

The girls that week, they were happy we'd made the playoffs, of course, but the way we'd made it? Just sneaking in? That was difficult for them. They'd gotten used to being the biggest dog, eh? But after Hayley got hurt? And then we'd lost our last two games? Suddenly we were no longer the big dog. Wade Central, *they* were the big dog, and we were the little puppy who had to go fight them.

That was a big change, psychologically. So that whole week getting ready for the playoffs, yes, we needed to fix some things on the field. But more important was fixing our heads. There was a lot of tension. A *lot* of tension.

High school kids... they're so young. They're dealing with things for the first time and, naturally, they don't always handle those things so well. If you were to ask Kaitlyn Baker about that week, she might tell you that she didn't handle things so well. Her passion, it was usually a good thing. But that week, it got the best of her, I think. There were some things she would probably want to take back. Especially concerning Chamique Lennox.

Kaitlyn Baker, central midfielder, team captain: I wasn't angry at Chamique. Far from it. She was just this kid who'd been thrown to the wolves. I didn't expect her to be Hayley Swanson. No one did.

My complaint was with everyone else. My complaint was with a back four who go from giving up three or four goals the entire *year* to giving up five goals over a game and a half. My complaint was with a defense that normally gave up maybe one shot over the course of an entire game, and now was giving up six, seven, eight shots on goal. Against a rookie keeper who is in no way equipped to face that.

That's what I was yelling about. Swanson goes down

and suddenly we forget how to play defense? Swanson goes down and suddenly our fullbacks can't close people out? Our center backs can't mark their friggin' man? It was ridiculous. Ridiculous.

So, yeah, I was hot. I did some yelling. Did I piss some people off? Sure. Fine. I didn't care. They needed to hear it. We were playing our worst soccer of the entire year, we'd barely snuck into the playoffs, and we were getting ready to play an undefeated team. We needed to get our heads out of our butts. And if it took a week of me yelling and screaming at everyone, fine. So be it.

Catalina Forero, center back: I wanted to kill Kaitlyn. Absolutely kill her.

What day was it when we got into that fight? I think it was Tuesday. Maybe Wednesday. She just wouldn't shut up, you know? She'd made her point. She'd made her point, like, fifty thousand times. And finally, I snapped.

It was right at the end of practice. We were scrimmaging and she was doing her usual thing, being the loudest voice on the field, and... What did she even say that made me snap? I can't remember. "Talk to Chamique," maybe. She was constantly on us. "Talk to Chamique, talk to Chamique, talk to Chamique," just non-friggin'-stop.

So finally, after like fifty thousand times of hearing it, I was like, "Jesus Christ, Kaitlyn, could you just shut up?" But super-loud, super-aggressive, you know? And I think I may have gotten up in her face, too. Did I get up in her face or did she get up in mine? It doesn't matter, we were there in the middle of the field, all up in each other's grills, loud as hell, shoving, screaming. There's girls pulling us apart, Coach is wading in, telling us to cool our heads. It was a scene.

[pauses]

But, you know, here's the thing... she was right. The back line, we were a mess. Those last two games, all those goals we gave up, those weren't Chamique's fault. That was on us. Me and Lisa and Estefania and Sylvia. Without Hayley behind us, talking in our ear, providing that calming voice... without that, we kind of fell apart a little.

So, yeah, I'll admit that Kaitlyn had a point. But that doesn't mean I wanted to hear her barking at me all week in practice. Hell, no. I had my pride. Lisa had her pride.

Actually, Lisa may have been even more annoyed, considering Chamique was her girlfriend.

Lisa Roney, center back: It was a tough situation for me. Very tough. And I didn't know how to handle it.

On the one hand, Chamique was suffering. Really suffering. She didn't want to be in that situation. She didn't want be thrown into goal with the whole season on the line. She'd joined the team so she could be the backup to the backup, not so she could be the starting keeper in a playoff game. So there we were, everything going to hell, everyone screaming at everyone else, and she's right smack in the middle of it. As her girlfriend, I thought I should protect her.

But, on the other hand, Kaitlyn was right. The back four was having serious problems. And what a time to have those problems, right? You'd think that, with a freshman thrown into the game, scared out of her mind, that's when we should have played *better*, right? You know, to help her survive. But nope. Instead we just got all confused and unorganized and flustered. All of us. Me, included.

That doesn't mean I wasn't annoyed with Kaitlyn. I was. Kaitlyn has a gift for that. She'd be like, "God almighty, this isn't rocket science! It's soccer! Do your friggin' job!" And I'd be like, "Back off, Kaitlyn! We'll handle it!" And she'd be like, "Then handle it! Now!"

It was brutal.

Estefania Higuain, left back: That whole week was horrible. The screaming, the yelling, the fights. I tried to stay out of it, but, you know... I was part of the defense. I was part of the problem.

We scrimmaged a lot that week. Coach Orostieta had us playing 12v11. You know, give the offense an extra man, put the defense under a little more pressure. I guess he figured if we could stand up to a 12-man team in practice, facing 11 players in the game would seem easy, right?

It's not like I didn't have enough going on in my life. I was still going straight from practice to the hospital. That week...

[pauses]

Jeez, after 10 years, you think it'd be easier to talk about, wouldn't you? Sorry.

[clears throat]

Hugo... that wasn't the week he died, but it's when things started going downhill. I mean *really* downhill. Fast.

[clears throat]

Yeah.

I was still going to the hospital, of course, but he was asleep most of the time. I'd talk to him when I could, but it wasn't often. I think we only spoke two or three more times.

[clears throat, wipes eyes]

But of course, those last few times, what did he want to talk about? The team. *[laughs]* I guess if you're going to die, you might as well go out thinking about soccer, right?

There was a lot to tell him. He loved the Kaitlyn stories, of course, and she was in a permanent bad mood that week, so I got to tell him about all that. I'd have to tell the stories quickly, though. He'd usually fall asleep in the middle of them. He was on a lot of medicine. Not that it was doing any good.

It was a tough week. A very tough week.

Chamique Lennox, goalkeeper: Honestly, I just tried to keep my head down. I was just trying to make it through those practices alive. Coach had me facing extra attackers. That was exhausting. Hayley, she was working with me, trying to get me ready, drill after drill after drill. That was exhausting, too. I was working my butt off.

So yeah, maybe after that first game when I gave up the three goals, maybe I came home and cried. But that passed. Eventually, I just put my head down, worked hard, and stayed out of all the drama. And there was a *lot* of drama. Kaitlyn and Catalina and Lisa? I didn't need to get involved with that. I had enough on my mind, thank you very much. Let them fight it out.

Hayley was a big help. It's pretty cool, you know, telling people that. During this last World Cup, I'd be watching a game with friends, and Hayley would be on TV, and I'd be bragging, telling them, "Oh, yeah, we worked together all the time. Really good friends. Besties." *[laughs]*

She was a genuinely good coach, though. I think she liked it. She seemed to, at least.

We did all the usual drills – you know, shot-stopping, distribution, that sort of thing – and that was all fairly decent, I guess, but the thing she kept harping on was communicating with the defense. She was like, "You gotta talk, Chamique. The defense needs you to talk to them, tell them what's up."

That was really hard for me. How could I tell Catalina and Lisa and Kaitlyn and all of them, how could I tell them anything? I didn't *know* anything. Barking out orders? I just couldn't do it. I needed the defense to talk to *me*, not vice versa. Hayley could harp on it all she wanted, but I was pretty much silent back there.

Ugh. What a mess of a week that was. Long, stressful, frustrating. I was almost glad when Friday came around and it was time to play.

Actually, that's not true. I was miserable. My stomach was in knots the entire day.

Carlos Orostieta, head coach: Our first round game was on the road, of course. Losing those last two games, we were the bottom seed, so all our games would be road games, no? This one, this was at Wade Central. A very big school about an hour north of us. Good team. Very good team. Won their conference three years running.

I called a coach I know, an old friend. He'd played

them that year, so I asked what he could tell me about them. That's about the best you can do for scouting. It's girls soccer, of course, so there's never any video to watch. There's never anything to read about them. I guess over the years we had a few articles about us in the Sycamore Times. After a state title, perhaps. Sometimes a feature story about a special player. But those were rare. A high school football team? A basketball team? They get a little more attention. They have scouting video to watch. But soccer coaches, we don't have much. That's the case with most high school sports, I'm sure. Especially the girls.

And when you don't know much about the teams you're going to play, what do you do? You work on yourselves. You worry about your own play. If you get your own team playing to their potential, then you'll be okay no matter what you face. That's the hope, anyway.

Catalina Forero, center back: It was a pretty long bus ride to Wade Central. I remember it being cold. Cold and clear.

After that crappy week of practice, I remember being pretty nervous, pretty pessimistic, but then when the game kicked off, things felt better. Just smoother, you know? Not Hayley-smooth, of course, but compared to those last couple games? Better. Calmer.

Chamique made a save in the first few minutes. Maybe 10 minutes in. It was on a header, I think. Yeah, I remember it now. Their forward, she was big. Strong.

Liked to use her head. She put up a hell of a fight all day. She was the one who had that first shot. A header, just inside the post. It totally could have been a goal. Actually, in Chamique's first two games, I think it *would* have been a goal. But this time, she was on it. Got over there and made a really nice save. Super-fast reaction, really stretched herself out, got a strong hand on it. Just a quality, quality save. A Hayley Swanson kind of save. In fact, I remember Hayley over on the sideline, yelling out to her. Something like, "Hell yeah, Chamique! You got this, girl! You got this!"

So, there we were, 10, 15 minutes in, and I'm actually starting to feel pretty good. The defense is feeling smoother, Chamique's making saves, building confidence, and I'm like, *Wow. Have we turned the corner? Are we back? We might be back. We might be able to win this.*

Kaitlyn Baker, central midfielder, team captain: It was the 20th minute when it happened. We had a corner kick and someone got their head on it. Lisa, maybe. She got her head on it, but didn't put it in. It may have gone off the post, actually. I'm not sure. What I do remember is that the ball was bouncing around the box for awhile. We were trying to kick it in, they were trying to kick it out, it was crazy.

Finally, one of their girls got a clean shot at it and kicked it just as hard as she could. Only problem? She kicked it straight into one of her own players and the ball ricocheted back into goal. An own goal!

11v11

So there we were, up 1-0. And who do you congratulate after an own goal? No one, really. So we just kind of jumped around and hugged each other, thankful for our good luck. I think I probably said something like, "Okay, girls, we've got our goal. That's all we should need. Let's win this thing." Something like that.

We kept that lead until halftime. I was really talking everyone up at halftime, really trying to build confidence. Especially with the defense. Telling Chamique she looked more comfortable, telling the back line they were looking like their old selves.

Maybe I was partially doing it to build *my* confidence up. Because I knew things were gonna get tougher in the second half. A lot tougher. Wade Central was a good team. The number one team in the state. They were gonna throw everything they had at us.

Carlos Orostieta, head coach: The second half... oh, my. It was like a hurricane. Wade Central, they were pushing forward, pushing forward, keeping us on our heels. I'm sure they had 75% possession in that second half. Maybe more.

When was the penalty? 50th minute? 60th minute? It was Catalina Forero getting called for a hand ball in the box.

Of course, it was a typical scene. After 40 years watching soccer from the sideline, I can tell you, my friend, most penalties are very similar. The referee, he's blowing his whistle and pointing to the spot. The defense is angry, the offense is happy. I usually didn't see everything, so I'm on the sideline, trying to figure out what happened, trying to get someone to tell me something. A few of my girls will be surrounding the ref, the other team will be wanting to take the shot, telling my players to leave the ref alone. The ref, he's pointing at the spot, telling everyone to clear out. *[laughs]* It is always the same, isn't it? When they go for you, you are thrilled. When they go against you, you feel the entire universe conspires against you. This is human nature.

So, in this game, the referee, he eventually quiets everyone down. The ball, it is placed on the spot, and Wade Central has a girl out there ready to shoot.

Oh my, you should have seen poor Chamique Lennox in goal. *[laughs]* She could not have looked more terrified, bless her. Hayley Swanson was next to me, yelling a few things to her – bits of advice – but really, at that point, it's up to Chamique. All we can do is watch. I'm sure I was standing there, already resigned to the game being tied up, already thinking how the rest of the game would play out. The score would be 1-1, and we'd have 20 minutes to try and find a goal.

But the girl, she misses! I can't remember which way Chamique dove – left, right, it doesn't matter – it was the wrong way. The Wade Central girl, she went the opposite way, the goal was completely open for her and she sent it wide! *[laughs]*

Well, I don't need to tell you, it was a huge bit of luck for us. Forero gets called for the handball, Lennox dives the wrong way, it should have been tied, but no, no, somehow we're still up, 1-0.

The question at that point? Could we hold on for another 20 minutes or so?

Estefania Higuain, left back: The rest of that game was *awful*. Wade Central, they just came at us and came at us, non-stop. I'm not sure I crossed midfield the rest of the game. I was just playing defense the whole time.

Their winger, she was really good. So fast, so aggressive. I wish I could remember her name. The two of us, we were going at it the whole game. They really liked attacking down that side, maybe because she was so good. I think I did a pretty good job against her, but still, they kept attacking and kept attacking. By the end, I was just exhausted.

Lisa Roney, center back: Playoff games are fun. Yeah, sure, they're exhausting and stressful and desperate, but all that stuff, it's kind of fun. Wade Central, they were desperate to score, we were desperate to hold them off. It's simultaneously horrible and fun. Maybe that's why we love sports, you know? That balance between awful and wonderful.

Anyway, we're holding them off, holding them off. Chamique, she'd had a few nice saves, which gave her confidence. The rest of the defense, we're surviving.

It's desperate. Fun, scary, awful, exhausting.

Eventually, we're in the 80th minute, and the ref says there's gonna be five minutes of stoppage time. I remember thinking that five minutes was a lot, but I didn't say anything. Kaitlyn Baker, though. *[laughs]* You better believe she said something. She was *furious.* You know how Kaitlyn is. So emotional. She just laid into the ref, told him he was crazy, told him it should've been three minutes, tops. You know, just being Kaitlyn.

So clock's ticking, clock's ticking, Wade's attacking, attacking, attacking. I think Chamique made another save. I remember someone blocking a shot. Catalina, probably. Clock's ticking, clock's ticking. I'm sort of halfway getting excited, halfway wondering why the ref hasn't blown his whistle yet. Defend, defend, defend. Absolute madness. I figure the ref's got to be right on the verge of blowing his whistle, and what happens?

Another penalty.

Catalina Forero, center back: Oh, dear God in heaven, don't get me started on that penalty. It's been ten years and it still pisses me off. Have you talked to Kaitlyn about it? She lost her friggin' mind over it. One of the worst calls I've ever seen, and I've seen a lot.

Okay, first of all, the game should've been over. Hayley was on the sideline, right? She told me she was looking at her watch the whole time. As soon as the game hit the 80th minute, she'd started the timer, and she says we'd already had six minutes of stoppage time. Six! So the game should've been over a full minute earlier. But no, that idiot ref kept us playing.

And then the call itself, are you kidding me? One, it was a dive. The girl clearly dove. No one touched her. And two, she wasn't even in the penalty box! She dives outside the box and the ref calls a penalty. Holy hell, what a call.

Well, no surprise, Kaitlyn Baker lost her mind. She was going *insane*. Right up in the ref's face, screaming, waving her arms, pointing at the ground, red in the face. It was amazing. Even by her standards, it was a world-class freak out.

And what happens? She gets tossed. Ref pulls out his red card and points to the sideline. Ejection.

At that point, *everyone* starts freaking out. I'm talking to the ref, Lisa's talking to the ref. I think the whole team had surrounded him, trying to convince him to put that red card back in his pocket. Because it meant Kaitlyn couldn't play in the next game. An ejection means a one-game suspension. If we win this game and make it to the semifinal, Kaitlyn can't play. So everyone's out there trying to talk the ref out of it. It's pointless, of course. No ref in the history of soccer has ever been talked out of a red card.

Kaitlyn... I remember her reaction, because it was so unlike her. When the ref pulled his red card, she went from freaking out to kind of... it was like she'd had the wind knocked out of her. Or like a bubble was popped. She realized, *Oh no, I just messed up big time.* And knowing her, she was also realizing, *I didn't just screw myself, I screwed my whole team.* And I remember, while the rest of us were surrounding the ref, Kaitlyn just walked over toward the sideline, her head hanging low. It was really something to see.

Well, anyway, I don't know how long we argued with the ref, but he's ignoring us, just pointing at the spot, and eventually, everyone realizes it's pointless. Kaitlyn's been tossed, the penalty's been called, and the ball's on the spot. Nothing to do but let them kick it and see what happens.

You know, I said the whole team was surrounding the ref, but that's not true. Chamique wasn't. She was just standing in goal looking miserable. Facing two penalties in one game? That's a tough day for any keeper, much less some freshman kid who's still figuring out how to play the position.

Chamique Lennox, goalkeeper: It was awful. *So* awful.

I mean, I was sure they were gonna score. *Sure* of it. Two PKs in one game? I'd gotten lucky on the first one. I'd totally guessed wrong, the girl had gone the opposite way, and I just got lucky that she missed. This time? No way would I get lucky again.

And secondly, once they tied it up 1-1, we'd have to play extra time – I think it's either an extra twenty or thirty minutes – and we'd have to play it a man down, because of Kaitlyn getting ejected.

So I was just as low as a person could be. Like, we'd really fought hard that whole game, you know? We'd faced a good team, we'd faced attack after attack after attack and somehow survived. And now, I was going to blow it for everyone. All that work was going to be for nothing.

That's pretty much where my head was when their girl was lining up to take the PK. Same girl who took the first PK.

Should I dive left? I'd tried that before and the girl had gone right. Dive right? The girl would know I'd do that, so she'd go left. So dive left? Right? I had no idea. My mind was completely locked up. Nothing I did would be right.

In the end, I just kind of stood there. I didn't dive left, I didn't dive right, I just stood still, completely frozen, completely unable to make a decision.

And she kicked it straight. Right into my belly. Easiest save anyone could ever make.

I was kind of in a daze, really. The ball was in my arms, teammates are hugging me, and the referee's blowing his whistle, telling us the game's over.

It was insane.

Catalina Forero, center back: I was losing my mind. Hugging everyone. I think I cried.

Estefania Higuain, left back: I was crying like a baby. I can admit it. It was just the release of emotions, you know? I'd been thinking about Hugo most of the game, so there was that. Plus, it was just a super-close game. Super-tense. And then, to cap it all off, a PK? *So* much drama. *So* much emotion. At the end, we were all holding our breath. So tense, so tense, and then – boom – Chamique makes the save. I just burst into tears. Freaking out, jumping around with everyone, tears pouring down. *[laughs]* It's kind of funny, looking back.

Carlos Orostieta, head coach: Everyone around me ran onto the field to celebrate. Even Hayley Swanson. *[laughs]* She's lucky she didn't re-injure her hand out there.

I suppose there was one player who didn't run out there. Kaitlyn Baker. She was over by herself, head hanging.

Kaitlyn Baker, central midfielder, team captain: I stayed on the sideline. I couldn't celebrate. The whole team was out there jumping around, but I couldn't join them. I didn't think I deserved to, you know? Not after what I did.

Man, I was in a bad place after that game.

Lisa Roney, center back: On the bus ride home, Kaitlyn apologized to the whole team. Stood up in the aisle and apologized for getting kicked out, for missing the next game. She was in tears, actually. I'd never seen her cry before. I didn't think she *could* cry, she was so tough. But there she was in the middle of this dark, quiet bus, talking about how she'd let the team down, how selfish she'd been, how sorry she was, and the whole time, tears were just streaming down her face. It was something else.

It tells you a lot about her, really. The team was *so* important to her. She usually showed that passion by playing hard. Harder than anyone else. But being suspended for the next game, she wouldn't be able to play hard. She wouldn't play at all. And it just gutted her. Just devastated her.

It's funny, there had been so much tension that year between her and Catalina. Between her and a lot of people, really. But if there had been any lingering resentments, any at all, they disappeared that night on the bus. Watching Kaitlyn stand there, sobbing, telling us how she'd let us down... jeez, how can you resent someone with that kind of passion?

I remember she said something like, "If you guys can get through the semifinal without me, if you can get us to the championship game, I swear to God, I will come back so strong. There won't be anything that can stop us. I swear. Just get us through this next game."

West Sycamore High School

Destinee Jones, left winger, team captain: The weekend after our win was pretty weird. I mean, we'd won, so that's awesome, right? Going to the semifinal? Should be party time, right?

Except, no. We'd lost our best player, we'd stunk up the entire second half, and just barely escaped with the win. So, no, that weekend was not a party. I think I spent most of the time wondering if we had any hope in hell of winning in the semis.

Jeez, one broken ankle and we go from being this great colossus to this scared little baby. I guess even the best teams have got their weak spot. Ours was Maria Solana. Take her off the field and we fall apart.

11v11

Nykesha Nolan, head coach: Monday morning, I was in my classroom, getting ready for first period, when who walks in but Maria Solana. Well, she doesn't walk in, she rolls in. Her ankle's in a boot and her leg's up on one of those scooter things with the wheels and the handle. Someone's with her to help translate. Yoreli Ospina, probably.

So, the room's empty and they come rolling in, and Maria tells me, "I want to help." She said it herself, in English. "I want to help." And she might have said, "But I don't know how." Something like that. Very simple English.

So, we sat down and talked for a while. Me, Maria, and Yoreli. We talked about the team, the win, how things went with Deavon Pope, with Susan Douglas. We talked for a while.

And to be honest, I kind of needed it. I needed that talk. I'd spent the whole weekend stressed right the hell out, wondering what I was going to do. I needed someone to bounce my ideas off. Someone who knew soccer. Someone I respected.

It just so happened that it was a 16-year old girl.

Maria Solana, central attacking midfielder: I remember, Coach, she was not her normal self that morning. Her normal self was so confident, so full of energy, but that morning, in the empty classroom, she was different. Very unsure. "I was thinking about doing this," she would say. "Do you think that is a good idea? What about this, should we try that?" She was asking me for my advice. Really asking.

I think that was the first time a coach had let me see the real them. Do you know what I mean? She took off her mask, I think. Her coaching mask. And then she was just a person looking for help. Someone who wasn't sure what to do.

We talked about using Susan Douglas in the middle. We talked about how Susan would play very different from me and so the rest of the team would have to get used to that. I told her we probably would not score as much. It would be a slower game.

Then she said, "Do you think you could work with her at practice? Help her get ready?"

This was a big surprise for me. And frightening, if I am being honest. How could I get Susan ready? I had never coached anyone. What would I do? Pull her off to the side so we could do drills? I couldn't do that, she needed to be on the field, practicing with the team. And would I have to pull Yoreli off the field, too, for the translations?

I think I smiled at Coach and tried to look confident, but as soon as I left the room, I told Yoreli, "I don't know how to coach. What am I going to do?"

That whole day, I was nervous and distracted. I didn't know what I would do that afternoon at practice. I was sure I would do it all wrong.

Clementine Thiamale, central defensive midfielder: Oh, my. What a week that was. Four days of long, hard practices.

Martha Sullivan, forward: Toughest week of the year, bar none. We were so stressed out.

Susan Douglas, central attacking midfielder: Yeah, that was a brutal week. Long practices, Coach completely stressed out, me trying to learn a new position. Coach was like, "Susan, do this. Susan, do that." Non-stop.

What she was really saying was, *Susan, be Maria Solana.*

Yeah, no problem, Coach. I'll get right on that.

Oh, and if that wasn't hard enough, she wanted me to be in two places at once. Seriously. She wanted Maria to work with me on the sideline – and that was a disaster, since Maria's English was so bad back then – but then Coach would be out on the practice field, yelling, "Susan, we need you out here!" I was like, *Jeez, Coach, make up your mind.* Back and forth, all day. It was stupid.

I guess it was only super-bad that first day. Those two must have gotten together and talked, because Tuesday was a little better. Maria worked with me before and after, but most of practice I was on the field, with the team.

That doesn't mean it was easy. Those practices were a meat grinder, start to finish.

Destinee Jones, left winger, team captain: Susan was working hard that week, no doubt. It was a tough spot for her. Trying to replace one of the best players in the world? I wouldn't want that job. Nobody would. But there she was, giving it her best shot. Coach yelling at her, Maria yelling at her.

The main thing you gotta know about Susan Douglas back then is that she didn't know how good she was. She was this quiet little girl. Meek. Had some of the best ball skills you can imagine. Give her a ball, all by herself, no one around, and she'd juggle that thing for hours. Put her out there with some friends, just goofing around, and she'd look like Mia Hamm. Like Neymar. Shooting, passing, dribbling, she could do it all.

But when the game started? When things got serious? She'd turn into this mousy little girl, not trying anything too difficult, nothing too dangerous. It frustrated the hell out of me.

Susan Douglas, central attacking midfielder: I wasn't as meek as everyone thought I was. Quiet? Yeah, sure. But that was by choice. And anyway, quiet's not the same thing as meek. I wasn't meek. I was tough. Losing your family will do that to you. Foster care will do that to you. It makes you tough. I makes you a survivor.

Maria Solana, central attacking midfielder: That first practice was bad, but things got better. Instead of trying to work with her during practice, Susan and I would talk a little before and a little after. I would tell her some things I saw, some things she could do differently, some things I would like her to try.

Susan Douglas was a nice girl, but very, very quiet. Even on the soccer pitch, she was quiet. But so good with the ball. Such a dribbler. At practice, she would juggle the ball in the air, just for fun, and keep it in the air for five, six minutes. On the field, she would play keep away from the other players. Two players would try to take the ball from her and she would dribble between them, keep the ball just out of reach. Like a magician. I was jealous of her dribbling. In games, when the defense came at me, I would pass the ball away, but Susan would dribble it away. That was the difference between us. I was a passer, she was a dribbler.

Susan Douglas, central attacking midfielder: Maria Solana's jealous of my dribbling? Wow. It's hard to imagine Maria Solana jealous of anyone. Gosh.

Well, dribbling or not, I knew I wasn't replacing her. Not perfectly, at least. I mean, jeez, she's Maria Solana. She's one of the best players in the world. Nobody could replace her perfectly. And who would want to try? I certainly didn't want the job. The whole team looking to me? Needing me to save the season? It was awful. The pressure was just terrible. Drill, drill, drill. Scrimmage, scrimmage, scrimmage. That's all we did that week. Maria was so huge for us. She did so much on both sides of the ball, replacing her was like starting from scratch. It was like starting a brand new team.

Thank God I was with the Galtons by then. If I'd still been bouncing between foster homes, it would've been too much. It would've taken a difficult week and made it completely impossible. I probably would've broken.

Nykesha Nolan, head coach: Susan and I had a few one-on-one conversations that season. Talking about her living situation, you know. She went through a lot that year. It was such a fun season for everyone else, but for her? Very tough.

That was my first year coaching, of course – my first year teaching – so Susan was my first kid with that kind of trouble outside of school. Not my last, not by any stretch, but my first.

When you sign up to be a coach, that's part of what you sign up for. Mostly it's about what happens on the field, on the court, on the diamond. But there's also the personal stuff. Because these are just kids, you know? They're almost adults, they want to be adults, they pretend they're adults, but they're not. Not yet. They're not quite sure how to do it. So you help them. A divorce? Drugs? Someone gets pregnant? Someone's dad gets arrested? They need someone to talk to. A lot of times, that someone is me.

Susan, she kept it all pretty quiet. We didn't talk a lot, but that was her choice. I checked in now and then, making sure it was all okay, but on the whole, she handled it her way. It was a tough year for her, but she was a tough girl.

Destinee Jones, left winger, team captain: After such a hard week of practice, it was almost a relief when Friday came. I wasn't sure whether to be confident or not – none of us were – but at least we could quit worrying. One way or the other, we'd find out.

The game was against Buchanan. Home game. Mom came. No Dad, no brothers. They had a football game. A playoff game, actually, same as us. Really, it's a little surprising Mom didn't go watch them. Good on Mom, eh?

The funny thing is, we were the better team that year. We were ranked #2 in the state, while football was ranked something like 7th or 8th. Our game was at home, theirs was on the road. So really, it should have been us getting all the attention, all the praise.

I guess we did get some. I remember, at school that day – Friday. Game day – there were actually a few people wishing me good luck, which was nice. I'm sure my brothers were getting more of that, but at least we were getting something, right? That was a new thing.

That was the week Maria won MVP, I think. Yeah, early that week. Monday or Tuesday. Maria won State Player of the Year and Coach won Coach of the Year. They announced it over the speaker. It was pretty cool. Made the whole team feel good. I remember seeing some of the girls in the hallway that day and being all like, "You hear that on morning announcements?" It was fun.

Of course, our Player of the Year had a broken ankle and our Coach of the Year was trying to make the team over from scratch, so that took some of the shine off of it, but, well, there you are.

Clementine Thiamale, central defensive midfielder: On game day, I remember Curtis walked me to the field. He and I were getting closer. How funny is that? All this stuff going on, all this tension, all this worry, and at the same time, Curtis and I are starting this romance.

I think we kissed that week. Yes, I'm sure of it. Tuesday or Wednesday. After school, but before practice. I'd been telling him how nervous I was about the team, and then we kissed and, oh boy, did that take my mind completely off soccer! *[laughs]* It's all very funny, looking back on it. So much going on. A very exciting time.

So yes, that's something I remember from the game on Friday. Curtis walking with me from the locker room up to the field. We held hands. The other girls teased me a little, but I didn't care.

Nykesha Nolan, head coach: It was a cold day. Maybe even a little misty, as I recall. Not rainy, but misty. Wet.

The game was against Buchanan. A home game, since we were the higher seed. Without Solana, though, I'm not sure we could be called the favorites anymore. We were like a brand new team, really. Who knew how we'd do?

Martha Sullivan, forward: You could instantly feel the difference. Everything was slower. More cautious. With Maria on the field, we pushed forward. Always forward. With Susan, we hung back. We played more defense. It's like we were an entirely different team.

I remember Daniela and I – that's Daniela DeLeon. She was usually the other forward – we were frustrated. The Buchanan defense, there were holes. There was space behind them I knew I could take advantage of. I'd be riding their back line, wanting to make the break, wanting someone to make the pass, but the pass never came. It was maddening. If Maria had been in there, she would have made that pass. She would have hit me over and over and over. I'd have bagged a goal or two by halftime.

But Susan? She just didn't see those opportunities like Maria did. And even if she did see them, she didn't have the confidence to make the pass. Maria *loved* making the hard pass. Loved it. Susan? She just... it wasn't who she was. And it was driving me up the friggin' wall.

Maria Solana, central attacking midfielder: Oh, yes, it was a very different game. We were a different team with Susan. Very different.

I was standing on the sideline with Coach Nolan, with my little scooter to rest my leg on. I saw plays that could have been made, goals that could have been scored, but I wasn't sure what to tell Susan. Should I tell her to try all the difficult passes? Was she ready? I don't think that she was. She was still very cautious. That is the word, yes? Cautious? Susan was so worried she would lose the game for us, that she was afraid to *win* the game for us.

In the end, I had to just let her play her way. Because, like I have told you, Susan was very skillful. She was very good at possession. At holding the ball. And that was important that day. Buchanan was getting frustrated. They were tired of chasing the ball around the field. And sometimes if you frustrate a team long enough, maybe they will give up a surprise goal.

Clementine Thiamale, central defensive midfielder: Being in a tight game was a new thing for us. All year, our offense had usually scored a goal or two by halftime, but not that day.

Susan Douglas was working her tail off. She was a really good dribbler, so I remember her playing a lot of keep away. Dribble here and there, make a short pass to me, a short pass to Destinee or Daniela or Deavon. I think I got more passes to me in the first half of that semifinal than I did in entire games with Maria Solana. Maria was always passing *forward*. Maria didn't want to make the safe easy pass back to me. She wanted to *score*.

But Susan wasn't Maria, so I got the ball a lot more that game. And we didn't run out to our usual big lead.

Destinee Jones, left winger, team captain: Yeah, it was a little frustrating. I mean, God bless Susan, she was doing the best she could, so, you know, I wanna be clear, I'm not ripping Susan. But that being said, yeah, I remember being a little frustrated. Because, you know, as soon as we'd get the ball into the final third, get ourselves into a good attacking position, it would just kind of peter out. The attack would just die. Over and over and over that happened.

It was a tough thing, having to change our whole style of play the way we did. We'd gotten used to being a race car, you know? And now we were an old broken-down jalopy, coughing and sputtering. *[thinking]* Okay, maybe not that bad. Maybe, like, a safe, boring car. A mini-van. We'd gone from being a race car to being a mini-van.

Martha Sullivan, forward: I'm a little ashamed to admit this, but... I didn't handle things as well as I could have that day. I was thinking about my stats. Thinking about scholarship offers. The Georgia Tech coach, she'd told me to call her. I knew she'd want to hear about all these goals I scored in the playoffs, and here I was with nothing. Not even a shot. That whole first half, we had opportunity after opportunity. Maria would've acted on them, but Susan wasn't, and it was driving me insane. The more passes Susan *didn't* make, the more frustrated I got, and the more I started thinking about my scholarship chances slipping away because Susan Douglas wasn't Maria Solana.

I'm not sure exactly when I blew up. First half. Maybe 30 minutes in? 35? I was doing all my usual things. Moving around their center backs, trying to be invisible, waiting for my chance. Susan would get a pass from someone, look up at me, and I'd think, *Okay, this is it*, and I'd break for goal. I'd time it perfectly, I'd be all alone, heading for goal, but no, Susan wouldn't make the pass. I don't know what she'd do with the ball. Something safe.

I was just getting angrier and angrier. Finally, after like the fourth or fifth time she *hadn't* made the pass, I come racing back up the field, yelling at her. I was like, "Dammit, Susan, I was wide open! How many times do I have to make that run before you hit me? Make the friggin' pass!"

I yelled it at her, right there in the middle of the field. She heard it, the defenders heard it, the ref heard it, the whole team heard it.

It was awful. I feel so bad about that, even now, 10 years later.

I mean, for starters, soccer's a team game. You shouldn't be out there thinking about your stat line. Secondly, don't yell at your teammate out loud like that. If you've gotta be angry, do it quietly. Don't do it so the whole world can see. And mostly, think about poor Susan Douglas. She didn't ask to be thrown into that situation. She didn't want everybody's hopes and dreams resting on her. I'm yelling at her because she's not Maria Solana? She knows she's not Maria. The whole world's been telling her how she's not Maria. Now I've got to do it, too? In the middle of a game?

Looking back, that might be my biggest regret of that whole season. Susan didn't deserve that. I was an ass, and I know it.

Destinee Jones, left winger, team captain: But at least we had our defense, right? They really picked it up. The whole back line played their tails off that day.

You know, I realize I haven't talked much about our defense, have I? They were kinda the forgotten half of our team that year. Which isn't too surprising, considering how great our offense was. Scoring three, four, five goals a game, it's easy to forget the girls in the back. But after Maria got hurt, oh Lord, did they have a bigger part to play.

So, let's see. There was Michelle Washington in goal. Good kid. Tall. Nice. I remember she and Clementine were good friends. That's a weird thing to remember after ten years, but for some reason I remember those two always together. They'd be over there talking French and stuff. It was cool.

Our right back was Yoreli Ospina. Nice girl. Thin. Fast. Connie Valenzuela was our left back. She was good, too. Not great. Nobody in our defense was *great*. But good? Sure. And in the playoffs, some of them came up great. They had no choice.

The two center backs were Tamika McKinney and Katrina Heinemann. Big girls, both of them. Tall. Maybe a little slow. But strong. Not afraid to bang. Tamika lived just down the street from me. I'd known her pretty much all my life.

So, yeah, that was our defense. They don't get the credit they deserve, since we were such an offensively-minded team, but lemme tell you, they came up huge at the end. Especially in that semifinal. Give 'em tons of credit. They really stepped it up.

Maria Solana, central attacking midfielder: It was a cold and rainy day. The field was getting sloppy. That is a word, yes? Sloppy? That is what the field was that day. Sloppy. And the girls were getting wet if they fell down or slid for a ball. The way Clementine played, I'm sure she was soaked.

At halftime the whole team, we went under the tent. There was a little tent we would go under at half. Not with walls, but just a top. Most games, the team, we would spread out, but that day everyone was cold and wet, so we crowded together under it.

A few girls, maybe they had a second uniform in their bag, so they would change into that. To be dry, you see. Or maybe putting on a long-sleeve undershirt to stay warm. The bench players were holding up their jackets so people couldn't see them changing. With my leg on my little scooter, I could not help with that.

I talked to Susan a little, telling her what I had seen, what she could do differently, but then I stopped. A lot of people were talking to Susan. Too many, I think. I could see that maybe we needed to stop. Maybe she didn't want to hear any more.

Susan Douglas, central attacking midfielder: God, halftime was awful. Everyone was on me. Advice, suggestions, demands. Coach was talking non-stop, telling me what she wanted in the second half. Destinee, too. Maria, she had the Latina girls translating for her, so I was getting yelled at in two languages. Martha Sullivan, she was the worst. She was like, "I'm open. I'm getting behind them. Make the pass."

And I'm sitting there in the middle of it, like, *Jeez, could you all just shut up and let me sit here for a minute? Catch my breath? Dry off a little?*

Nope, I'm surrounded and they're piling the weight of the whole team on top of me. Like I *asked* for the job or something. I never wanted to lead that team. Never. It just sort of happened.

At a certain point, I just stopped listening. I'm sure I nodded my head and acted like I was listening, but no, I just shut down. You can only take so much.

[pauses]

You know, in a way, that's kinda how the rest of my life

was, too. Mom turning up dead, Grandma dying, foster home, foster home, foster home. After awhile, you're like, *Jeez, life, could you just shut up for awhile? Let me catch my breath?*

So you go inside yourself and you think, *You know what? All this noise outside me, all this awful stuff happening, that's not me. Deaths, foster homes, none of that I can control. Here inside my head, that's the only thing I can control.* So you shut your ears, you pick your head up, and you carry on.

That's what I had to do with my home life, and that's what I did in that soccer game. I tuned out all the noise, I went out onto the field, and I played my game. Not Maria's game. *My* game. Cause that's the only game I could play.

Martha Sullivan, forward: The second half was interesting. Things shifted. Momentum started swinging our way. Not because we changed. Susan didn't start charging down the field. She didn't start making Maria Solana passes.

What changed was Buchanan getting tired. The entire first half, they'd been chasing the ball. Susan dribbles away from pressure, they chase. Little tiny passes to Destinee and Deavon and whoever, Buchanan has to chase. Chase the ball, chase the ball, that's pretty much all they did that whole game. And that wears your legs out, you know? So in the second half, Buchanan started getting tired. You could see it happen. They weren't going after the ball quite so hard. Their legs were just a little slower. And as soon as that happened, things started improving for us.

I think I got my first shot off in the 50th minute. Somewhere around then. I can't remember the play. I was riding the back line, probably, trying to get behind the D, and finally, after so many times *not* getting the pass, I get it. Didn't score, but hey, a shot's a shot, right? It's a start.

I think I had two more in the next ten minutes. Our bench sees what's happening, they start cheering like crazy. The Buchanan girls, they see it, too, and they get this worried look, like, *Oh, Lord, don't let this game get away from us.* They're tired, we're energized. All the momentum's on our side.

Nykesha Nolan, head coach: When did it happen? 70th minute? 75th? Right near the end. Buchanan was tired, getting desperate. They had the ball, pressing forward, trying to get a goal. We're backing up, playing D, and then suddenly, the ball comes off someones head, takes this long carom back upfield, and lands at Sullivan's foot. Boom! We've instantly got a 3-on-2 fast break.

You know how those counters are, everyone on the bench is immediately yelling, "Go, go, go!" It was Martha Sullivan, Susan Douglas, and Destinee Jones. Jones is hauling ass down the left side, Douglas and Sullivan are in the center, and I'm just praying we don't mess it up. Because, you know, if Solana's on the field, it's almost a guaranteed goal. But with Douglas? Who knows? Will she be aggressive? Will she trust herself to make the difficult play? No one knew.

So, the bench is screaming and yelling, the ball's getting toward Buchanan's box, and it's reached the point where Susan Douglas has to make a decision. What's she gonna do? Pass to Jones on the left? Sullivan on the right? Take it herself? Freeze up, so no one gets a shot? I remember it like it was yesterday. I was like, *Oh, please, Susan, don't get shy, don't play it safe.*

And she didn't. Maybe it was the work she'd done with Maria, maybe it was all my yelling, telling her to be aggressive, but she made the hard play. She faked shooting it herself, just a little fake, and the goalie bit. Then Susan made a little outside-of-her-foot pass to Sullivan in the middle, and the goalie's so out of position from the fake shot, Sullivan just taps it in.

Great play, start to finish, and, honest to God, a huge breakthrough for Susan. She made the hard play and it paid off. A huge moment for her. For the whole team, really. We'd finally scored a goal without our best player, and we'd done it with a really nice play from her replacement.

Maria Solana, central attacking midfielder: On the sideline, I fell over. I was so happy, I was crying, and I went to hug someone – I don't know who – and I fell off my little scooter, down onto the wet grass. The whole thing was funny, looking back. The girls were picking me up, we were all smiling and laughing, and I was all wet from the ground. It was a very happy moment for all of us. That game, it was so tense. We were all so nervous. So scared. And finally, late in the game, to score like that, oh, what a relief! Those are the best games, I think. Not the ones you win 5-0, but the hard ones, the scary ones. That is where the real joy is.

At the beginning of the year, I didn't know what they meant by *State*. "We could win State," they said, and I would smile and nod like I knew what it meant and how exciting it was. But now I *did* understand it. The team was going to play for the state championship, and I was so, so excited. I wouldn't be playing, of course, because of my ankle, but I was still excited. I could still help the girls get ready. I could still be a part of the team.

East Sycamore High School

Carlos Orostieta, head coach: The week leading up to the semifinal, that was an interesting week, I can tell you. Many different emotions. Some good, some not so good.

The team was happy to still be playing, of course, but the win over Wade Central? It was far from dominant. A lucky win, you could call it. And that was a new feeling for the team. After being so dominant for so much of the season, now they were having to shift their thinking. And that was a challenge, you see. They were trying to think of themselves as just another team, eh? Not the best team in the state, not a team with all the future professionals, all the future World Cup players, but just another team. That was a new feeling for them. And it made for a difficult week of practice.

Catalina Forero, center back, team captain: That week was funny, because, you know, we'd spent the previous few weeks getting ready to play without Hayley, but now it was all about getting ready to play without Kaitlyn.

I knew I'd be wearing the captain's armband, of course, but I gotta be honest, I barely wanted it. I would much rather have had Kaitlyn playing. I mean, she *ran* that midfield. Yeah, sure, she'd gotten tossed from games before, so we'd played a game or two without her, but those were regular season games, against teams we could beat with our eyes closed. Plus, we'd had Hayley Swanson in goal.

Now? In the state semifinal? Against the fourth-ranked team in the state? On the road? With a freshman in goal? It was a scary situation. We spent the entire week of practice getting ready for it.

Carlos Orostieta, head coach: Replacing Kaitlyn was difficult. I decided to go with Mary Ogwumike, who was our left winger. Mary, she was a good girl. Solid on offense and defense. Not the player Katilyn was, but still the best choice, I thought. Filling in for Mary at left wing, I had Mona Nash. Big girl, strong girl. Not the best feet, kind of a hard touch, but a wonderful athlete. Very fast.

So, yes, that's what we did in practice that week. Get the team used to Ogwumike in the center of the pitch instead of Baker. Get Nash ready on the left side. It was a difficult week, I can tell you that.

You know, after 40 years coaching, you'd think my last year would be easy, wouldn't you? *[laughs]* You'd think I could spend those last few weeks relaxing, eh? Sipping a drink? Watching all my starters get ready, all my all-stars get ready?

But, no. That is not what the universe had in store for me. "You are going to have to work, Carlito!" That is what the universe said. "You think this should be easy?" *[laughs]*

No such luck, eh, my friend? If I wanted to win one last championship, I was going to have to work for it.

Kaitlyn Baker, central midfielder: That was an awful week. I can't tell you how angry I was at myself. Such a stupid red card. Just stupid.

You know, you want to be passionate. You want to care. But there's a line, right? There's a point past which you're not being passionate, you're just being an idiot. And I crossed that line. The ref, he messed up – twice – and I just kind of lost it. The red mist descended.

Have you heard that expression? *The rest mist descends?* I don't know where it's from, but I like it. Because that's what it feels like, you know? Like red is all you can see. That girl, with her friggin' dive. The ref, totally falling for it. The red mist descends, and I lose my mind. Get tossed. Completely unacceptable.

Completely unacceptable.

But anyway, that was past. What mattered now was getting the team ready to play without me. So there I was at practice, working with Mary Ogwumike, working with everyone else, doing what I could.

I didn't like it. Coaching's not for me. I want to be out there on the field. Talking to people? Watching? Giving pointers? I hated it. Hayley Swanson, she was better at it than me. She actually seemed to enjoy coaching Chamique. Me? I hated it. I probably did more harm than good. I don't know.

Estefania Higuain, left back: Yeah, practices were tough that week, but I was only there for a couple of them. I missed the first part of the week. Hugo's funeral.

He died Sunday night. Maybe Monday morning. It was at home. Did I tell you he came home to die?

He'd been at the hospital for awhile, but nothing there was working. All the things they were trying, none of it helped. At a certain point, someone decided that if he was going to die, he should do it at home, with his family.

[clears throat]

I don't know who makes that decision. The doctors, my parents, someone. Not me, thankfully. I can't imagine. Deciding, *Oh, we've done all we can do. It's time to let him die.* What a decision to have to make! I imagine it's the doctor who decides that. My parents, they probably decided he should die at home. Among family.

So that was Saturday. There were hospice workers who came to the house every day to check on him. Give him morphine. At that point, it was just about reducing his pain. They weren't trying to keep him alive.

That's another thing I don't think I could do. Be a hospice worker. Help people die. I think my heart would break every single day. God bless them for doing it, but I don't think I could. They're stronger than me.

Anyway, that's what was going on in my life that week. Hugo dying. His funeral.

[clears throat, wipes eyes]

It kind of puts the playoffs in perspective, doesn't it? Hard to get too stressed about the semifinal when you're watching them put your brother in the ground.

Lisa Roney, center back: Game day, it was cold and rainy. Friday, of course, just like the rest. Road game, just like the rest. I sat with Chamique on the bus. She was quiet. Nervous.

The game was against East Poe. 4th seed, I guess they were. I remember they had a really good striker. I wish I could remember her name. Big and tall. Could jump through the roof.

Their defense was good, too. Just a good all-around team. If we'd met them during the season, when we were full strength, we'd have been the favorites. But without Hayley? Without Kaitlyn? We were clearly the underdog. In fact, I think most people would've called it a mismatch. Most people expected us to get blown out.

But that's why you play the games, right?

Carlos Orostieta, head coach: Our offense that year, it was never all that good at creating. But with Kaitlyn Baker out? Oh, my.

So I thought, *Why sit back and absorb pressure? Why not take the game to them?* I told my girls to attack them way up the field. Especially my forwards. Hound their back line, hound their goalie, get some turnovers high up the field, hopefully turn them into goals. That was my plan. And it was a good plan. I just didn't expect it to bear fruit so quickly.

I guess Mona Nash wanted to impress me, no?

Catalina Forero, center back, team captain: It was super-early in the game. Maybe third minute. Rain's coming down, field's sloppy. We're still getting our legs under us, really. The play, it happened way down at the other end of the field, of course, but I had a pretty good view of the whole thing.

Ball was over on the left side. My left. An East Poe player – their winger, I guess – she was getting harassed by someone. That high pressure Coach was asking for. So their girl, she's passing it backward, back to her fullback or her center back or someone. Just sending it somewhere safe. Somewhere out of trouble.

But with us turning up the high pressure? Nowhere was safe.

Truth is, when I saw the ball heading toward their center back and saw Nash racing back there after it – just *racing* after it – I didn't realize it was her. She didn't play a lot, so I wasn't used to seeing her on the field. I thought it might be Gloria Cayetano or Vilma Aguilar. But no, it was Mona Nash, just racing up the field, chasing after that ball.

Mona was on the track team. A sprinter, I think. Fast. Not the best soccer player, but as a pure athlete? Great.

So anyway, their center back, she collects the pass, but then, instead of sending it over to the other center back or just clearing it out of there, she sees Mona bearing down on her – big, strong, fast, scary Mona – and she kind of goes stupid for a second. *[laughs]* It's funny, looking back on it. It was a total mess. You could actually see her realizing, *Oh, hell, I better get rid of this ball.* She puts her foot to it, but it was too late. Nash kinda threw herself forward, sliding through the wet grass, water sloshing everywhere. The defender kicked it, Nash's foot was right there, the ball hits it and goes like a rocket straight toward goal. The goalie dives for it, but there's no chance. Goal. 1-0, just like that. *[laughs]*

Mona was jumping around, going crazy. Everyone was. There was a big mob of girls up there, all hugging each other. Same on the sideline. Kaitlyn's in her street clothes, so excited, giving everyone high fives. Three minutes in, and we're up 1-0. It was a great scene. I've got goosebumps just describing it for you.

Chamique Lennox, goalkeeper: We were going bananas. I was in the back with Catalina and Lisa. We were out there in the rain, hugging each other, jumping around, just freaking out. Early goals, man, there's nothing like them. I mean, goals at any point are awesome, but a goal like that? Super early in the game? On such a crazy play? It was like a shot of adrenaline.

So, there we were, fourth or fifth minute, already up 1-0. East Poe's kicking off, Catalina's yelling at everyone, "Focus! Focus!" You know, trying to keep everyone straight. We still had 75 minutes to play. You don't want to let your guard down, right? Don't want to give up a quick goal. So that's what Catalina was yelling. Hell, we all started yelling it. Me, Catalina, Coach, everyone. "Focus! Focus!"

Carlos Orostieta, head coach: But as it turned out, I didn't need to worry, eh? Such a group of girls! They pulled themselves together, no problem. I remember watching them from the sideline, hiding under my umbrella, and thinking, *My heavens, they look good.* Getting that early goal could've gotten them all scatterbrained, but it didn't. I think it gave them confidence, really. Made them believe. Believe they could do it.

Estefania Higuain, left back: That was a weird game for me. I was kind of out of it the whole time. Probably because of Hugo. Well, not probably. Definitely. Definitely because of Hugo. We'd only buried him a couple days earlier, so I was still kind of a mess.

I remember kind of wandering around the field, thinking about him, and then I'd look up and be like, *Oh, wait, there's a game going on? Did I miss anything?* That's what it was like.

I guess it sounds kind of funny, telling it to you 10 years later, but at the time it wasn't funny at all. It made me angry. I remember thinking, *Come on, Estefania. This is unacceptable. You need to play well for Hugo.* You know, sort of in honor of him? But I *wasn't* playing well. I was drifting in and out of the game. Really scatterbrained. And it felt like an insult to Hugo. I remember being really annoyed with myself about that.

The rest of the team was playing well, at least. We had the early goal. The *two* early goals, I suppose. 20th minute, that's early, right?

Carlos Orostieta, head coach: It was a lovely team

goal.   The   prettiest   goal   we   scored   that   whole
postseason, I would say.

It started in the back with Catalina Forero and her long
cross-field pass to Ye-Jee Park.   Ye-Jee, she raced
down the right side, heading toward the corner.   Her
girl came out to shut her down, of course, but the field
was very wet, very sloppy, and the girl fell down, so
Ye-Jee had time to look up and pick her spot.

She passed to Mary Ogwumike just outside the box.
Mary took one soft touch, then passed to Gloria
Cayetano in the box, at the penalty spot, roughly.   She
had her back to goal, her defender all over her.   As soon
as Mary passed to her, she cut straight for goal and
Cayetano tapped it back to her.   Wonderful give-and-
go.   Mary didn't pause, just one-timed it into goal.
Their poor goalkeeper, she didn't have a chance.   So I
believe it was Forero to Park to Ogwumike to Cayetano
to Ogwumike to goal.   Bang, bang, bang, bang, bang.
[laughs] Goals that pretty, you don't see them too often
in high school soccer, I can tell you.   I was so proud of
my girls.

Chamique Lennox, goalkeeper: It's funny, the things
you remember.   After that second goal, we were all
there in front of goal.   The defenders, I mean.   Me,
Lisa, Catalina.   We were all hugging and laughing.   It
was raining, so we were wet from that.   And I
remember we were in this little huddle, our foreheads
sort of pressed together.   Catalina was saying soccer-
type things.   You know, "We got this.   Stay focused.
Game's not over."   That sort of thing.

But Lisa's not saying that. She's just got her forehead pressed against mine, and she's looking at me with these eyes. You know, girlfriend eyes. Loving eyes. And when our little huddle broke up, our three-person huddle, she gave me a little kiss – just a little one – and whispered, "I believe in you."

It's kind of a random thing to remember, I guess, but... I don't know... it was just the sweetest thing ever, and I remember it to this day. The eyes. The kiss. What she said. It was all really, really sweet, and I think it helped me the rest of the game. I really do.

Gosh, look at me, getting all teary-eyed. *[wipes her eyes, laughing]* I'm such a sap.

Estefania Higuain, left back: It was all such a surprise. Up two goals after only 20 minutes? None of us expected that. So the whole team was buzzing with the excitement of it. Even me. I mean, I was still kind of out of it, thinking about Hugo and all, but gosh, 2-0? How could I not be excited?

But then everyone started yelling, "Focus! Focus!" You know, Coach on the sideline. Kaitlyn and Hayley. Catalina. Everyone. That was, like, the theme of the game. Stay focused. Don't let up. All of that.

Which was smart, because the game was *far* from over. There were still 60 minutes to play. And, like, didn't we give up three goals in one half just a couple weeks earlier? Three weeks earlier? So yeah, we needed to stay focused. Especially me, out there sleepwalking, thinking about Hugo's funeral. I *needed* people yelling at me to focus.

And it must have worked, because the team looked really good that day. We held possession, we didn't get flustered. Chamique was better in goal. Front to back, the team was solid. It was nice. It's like we were our old selves again.

Kaitlyn Baker, central midfielder: It was a strange feeling, watching the team play so well without me. It was hard, to be completely honest. Very hard. Because that was definitely our best game of the playoffs, right? And it happened with me on the sideline. Did it happen *because* I was on the sideline? I didn't know.

I wish those thoughts hadn't been in my head. I was standing there with Coach and Hayley and all the bench players, and I was trying to enjoy things, enjoy our great play, but it was tough, with all those questions in the back of my mind. I was, you know, a 17-year-old kid. I had my insecurities, just like everyone that age does. So even though I was cheering and high-fiving and mostly enjoying the game, trust me, there was some real uncertainty in the back of my head. *Does this team even need me? Are they better without me?*

Carlos Orostieta, head coach: East Poe, they pulled a goal back, but it was very late in the game. 70th, 75th minute, sometime around then. It was a mess of a goal, I can tell you that. One of our defenders – Catalina or Lisa, I suppose – they tried to clear a ball, but with the field so wet and messy, they accidentally hit it straight up in the air. When the ball came down, it landed right at someone's foot, right there in front of goal. It was pretty much a tap-in.

But of course, goals like that happen, don't they? In the third minute, their center back gave us a gift. In the 75th, our center back returned the favor. Such is life. Such is soccer.

That made the score 2-1. Those last five minutes were tense, definitely. East Poe came at us, came at us, we cleared the ball deep a few times, took the ball into the corner a few times, and then the game was over. We were heading to the championship game.

A 2-1 victory without our captain? With our third-string goalkeeper? In the cold and rain? I think most coaches would take that, don't you think?

It was probably the best game we played that entire postseason, and if I told you I had expected it, I would be lying.

Chamique Lennox, goalkeeper: The bus ride home was a party. Cheering, yelling, singing songs. Lisa and I were cuddled up in our seat, all muddy and gross. It was wonderful.

That was the first game I felt genuinely good about my performance. Like I deserved to be the starting goalkeeper. The previous game, against Wade Central, yeah, sure, I'd gotten the shutout, but I didn't deserve it.

I'd faced two PKs, guessed wrong on the first, froze on the second, and gotten lucky both times. So, no, I wasn't proud of that, even if it was a shutout.

But the East Poe game? I'd done well. I'd made a couple nice saves, my distribution was good, I was talking maybe a tiny bit more. And the goal we gave up, that was a fluke goal. That wasn't my fault. So, yeah, I came out of that game feeling pretty good about myself.

Just in time, too. Because, look out, here comes the championship game. And here comes West Sycamore, who were only the best offensive team in the state. If there was ever a team that could score some goals, it was them.

So yeah, I was happy about the win, I was happy about playing well, but in the back of my mind, I was already thinking about facing West. I was gonna need to play my best game yet. And I had a week to get ready.

West Sycamore High School

Nykesha Nolan, head coach: That next week was nuts. I was so stressed out. Is stressed the right word? Overwhelmed might be better.   I just remember thinking, *God almighty, Nykesha, how did you end up here? Never played a game of soccer in your life, and suddenly you're coaching a team in the state championship. How?* That was kind of my feeling the entire week.   Disbelief.   Disbelief that it was really happening.

Carlos Orostieta, he'd been doing it for, what, 40 years? How many championships had he gotten ready for? 10? 15? He wasn't freaking out, but I sure was.

I think I faked my way through it pretty good, though. I don't think the girls could tell I was freaking out inside.

I ran practices about the same as always and they went smoothly. Drills, scrimmages, the whole thing. After winning a game with Susan Douglas in the middle, I was feeling a whole lot better about that. She was, too. And, of course, I still had Maria Solana helping me out with that. She worked with Susan before and after practice. That helped.

So, yeah, it was a good week. A little nerve-wracking, but on the whole, good.

Martha Sullivan, forward: That was the week I got offered a scholarship. Yep, a full ride to play college soccer. Pretty sweet, right?

The only problem? The offer wasn't from Georgia Tech, it was from Colorado State, my second choice.

I think the call came on Monday or Tuesday. It was their coach. He was super-excited, told me congratulations, all that stuff. Said I was going to be a big part of their team moving forward. It was incredibly cool.

I remember, I was in the kitchen when he called. My sister was there, too, but she didn't know who it was or what we were talking about, she just saw my face burning bright red, this huge smile on my face. As soon as I hung up with him, she was hitting me up, asking me what was going on. It was all very exciting.

But still, it was weird. Because, like I said earlier, I'd kind of gotten my heart set on Georgia Tech. Once I'd done that, I'd started imagining myself living in Atlanta, living in a big city. And, yeah, both schools have computer science programs, but you know, once you get your heart set on a particular outcome, once you start daydreaming about it, imagining yourself living that life, it's hard to immediately switch gears, immediately give up that dream and start dreaming something new.

So in the end, I put them on hold. On the phone, he was like, "All I need from you is a commitment, Martha. Can I mark you down for Colorado State?"

And I was like, *Oh, jeez, what do I do? What do I do?*

In the end, I think I said something like, "You know, I need to talk to my parents first. Can I get back to you?"

He said some stuff about how he hoped I wouldn't make him wait too long, he had other players he was interested in, he couldn't hold my scholarship forever. That last part was the worst. *He couldn't hold my scholarship forever.* I almost crumbled at that point and said, *Yes! Yes! I'll take it! Yes!* But I didn't. I told him I'd get back to him.

That was agony. It really was. The rest of that week, I was wondering if I'd made the worst decision of my life. What if Georgia Tech didn't call? What if I screwed up in the championship game? Screwed up so bad that, not only would Georgia Tech not want me, but Colorado State would take back their offer. Tell me the deal was off. What then?

It's crazy, right? All year long I'd been trying to get a scholarship. When I finally do get one, I tell them I have to think about it, then spend the rest of the week wondering if I'm the stupidest person who ever lived.

Destinee Jones, left winger, team captain: It was a good week of practice. A confident week. Sure, we were a little nervous, how could we not be? But mostly, we were feeling good. We'd had a good win without Maria Solana, so that was nice. Plus, East Sycamore was a little banged up, too. Not having to face Hayley Swanson? We had to feel good about that.

I remember being pretty excited that my family was gonna come watch. Oh, yeah, the whole gang. The football team had lost their playoff game, so their season was over. With no game to play on Friday, the boys were gonna come cheer me on. Dad, too. I was so pumped.

It's funny, Dad saw me play exactly two times that year, and both games were against East Sycamore. And, come to think of it, both were without Maria Solana. The first time, we'd lost 1-0, and he'd been grumbling about how boring soccer was. This time, though? One, it was for the state championship, and two, no Hayley Swanson in goal. Damn, I couldn't wait! A backup keeper? I was sure we'd score some goals. Sure of it.

I thought about that a lot during practice that week. *Dad's coming. Let's put on a show for him. Let's score two, three, four goals. Show him soccer's fun. And hell, as long as we're at it, let's win State.*

Clementine Thiamale, central defensive midfielder:
I think it was Wednesday or Thursday when Curtis
came over for dinner. My parents insisted. If I was
going to have a boyfriend, they wanted to meet him.
To approve of him.

He was scared, of course, which is understandable. I
was scared, too. A boy meeting my family? Coming to
my house? That's scary for any girl, I think. Curtis was
wondering if my parents would approve of him, but I
was wondering if Curtis would approve of *them.* If he
would approve of *me,* once he saw me at home with my
family.

The real question, of course... my real fear... *were my
parents too African?* Because, of course they were. Of
course they were too African, with their clothes and
their accents and their... just their way of being. I was
terrified they'd embarrass me. Curtis was a nice
American boy. Oh sure, maybe he thought it was cool I
was from Cote d'Ivoire, and he thought my accent was
cute, but when he came to my house? Met my family?
Would it all be too overwhelming?

Mama was planning this big meal with all her favorite
Ivoirian foods. Kedjenou, fufu, calalou, cornmeal
cookies. I was like, "No, Mama, he'll hate it. Can't we
have something American?" But she wouldn't hear a
word of that. It was awful. I was so scared.

I remember that day, waiting for him to arrive. I was

going around the house and sneakily hiding things that I thought were too African. Like this one little statue my papa had in the hallway. A statue of a person. Knee-high. Carved wood. Some sort of tribal thing. I hid it. Put it in a closet.

It's strange coming to a new country. Most of the time you don't mind being different, but every now and then, you have these moments where you wish you could just be American. Just another normal, boring American kid. That's how I was feeling that week, thinking about Curtis coming to my house, meeting my family. It was awful.

Maria Solana, central attacking midfielder: It was a difficult week for me, watching the team get ready. I was helping Susan a little. I was talking with Coach Nolan a little, helping her plan for the game. But none of that is what I wanted to do. I wanted to play. I wanted to practice with the team, I wanted to play in the game, I wanted to be on the field. It was very frustrating.

Still, I loved the team. I would do what I could.

Susan, she was feeling much better about playing in the middle. Much more confident. That was nice. I worked with her a little before and after the practices. Even in English, sometimes. My English lessons, they were helping. Me and my family, we were trying so hard to become American. Learning English, doing American things.

I think that was the week I went bowling. Wait, it was not bowling, it was the golf thing... what do you call it? Little golf? Mini golf! Yes, that's it. Mini golf. Except Yoreli, she called it something else. Putt-putt? Yes, putt-putt. That was the week I did putt-putt with Yoreli and her family.

I didn't know what it was, of course. My town in Colombia, I told you how small it was. We didn't have such things. If I had grown up in Cali or Bogota or some big city like that, I probably would have known about putt-putt, but no, I didn't. I remember Yoreli telling me it was a very American thing. People do it all the time. So, of course, I was interested. I wanted to do American things. So I went.

I didn't do well. I had the little scooter thing for my leg, of course, so I was pushing myself around on that. Then I had to figure out how to use the golf stick without falling over. I remember we were laughing about how hard it was for me. We were trying to figure out, should I swing the stick with one hand? Two hands? Should I try to stand while Yoreli held me up? It was very funny trying to do it. And Yoreli's family, they were very nice.

I've told you how it is sometimes hard to be an immigrant, but then there are other times when being an immigrant is fun. All these new things, they can be very exciting. They can make you fall in love with your new country. You start to think, *Oh, I could be happy here. I could be an American. I can do American things.*

That is a funny thing to remember from that week, yes?
The team was getting ready for the championship game,
and I was learning how to do putt-putt.

Clementine Thiamale, central defensive midfielder:
In the end, dinner with Curtis was great. He was so
sweet. He could barely understand my papa's accent.
[laughs] And, of course, Papa was trying to be all
scary, but he wasn't very good at it. In the end it was
more funny than anything. And Mama, she was just as
nice as could be. Curtis loved her.

Oh, and the food, he *loved* the food. Well, maybe not
the fufu, as I recall, but everything else, he just went on
and on about it. So Mama liked that.

I don't remember it all perfectly, but I do remember that
at a certain point, I was like, *Oh, this is going to be
okay, isn't it? This is working. My family, we're not the
perfect American family, but we're okay. Being
African's okay.*

That's a nice thought to have.

Susan Douglas, central attacking midfielder: That
was a good week. People really got off my back. The
week before, everyone had been like, *Oh, God, we're
doomed! We've lost Maria! We can't win with Susan!
This is going to be so awful!*

But then we did win. We beat Buchanan with me in the
middle, and it gave us some real confidence. Suddenly,

everyone was like, *Oh, we're not doomed. We* can *win with Susan. We can play a different style and still win.*

I was working with Maria before practice, after practice, and she'd stopped trying to get me to play the same as her. Instead, it was more like, *Okay, we know playing your way works, Susan, so let's get that all polished up.* It was a nice change.

The plan was to try and wear East Sycamore down, same as we'd done with Buchanan. Control possession, hold the ball, play keep-away, make them chase us, tire them out. During scrimmages that week, Coach would be yelling at us from the sideline, "Hold the ball! Hold the ball!" If someone tried a pass that was a little too long? Like say a center back was clearing the ball deep, way upfield, Coach would be on the side yelling, "No, no, no! Short passes! Hold the ball! Control it!"

She never would have said stuff like that with Maria in the middle, because with Maria we were a different team. But with me? Holding the ball was our best bet.

That was the plan, at least. We didn't actually know how things would play out once the game started. Would holding the ball work against East Sycamore? Maybe they were too good to play keep-away against. There was no way to know until game time Friday night.

East Sycamore High School

Carlos Orostieta, head coach: It was a good week of practice. Very good. After such a strong win over East Poe, the girls, they finally felt like *themselves* again, yes? Finally felt like the team they'd been all season, when Hayley Swanson was in goal.

Chamique Lennox, she'd given up a goal, yes, but it wasn't really her fault. She could take some pride in that. The midfield? Mary Ogwumike? Vilma Aguilar? They'd won a game without Kaitlyn Baker. And won it handily, thank you very much. So they could take some pride in that.

Yes, it was a good week of training, a good week. Which was nice, I think, after feeling so uncertain for so long.

Of course, we were going to play a very, very good team in West Sycamore. We'd beaten them in the regular season, so that gave us confidence. Yes, their star player had been out that day, but she would be out again for the championship, wouldn't she?

That was a shame, really. Maria Solana, what a player! And such a nice girl, too. Have you met her? It's a shame she couldn't have been healthy for the championship. Such a shame. But then again, we were missing our goalkeeper, so perhaps it was a wash? Yes, I think so. A great defensive team missing its keeper, a great offensive team missing its playmaker? I think in the end, that balances out.

It was a good matchup. Offense against defense. I had a week to get them ready.

Kaitlyn Baker, central midfielder: That was a really hard week for me personally. The team had looked so damn good playing without me. It really got in my head. Really messed me up inside.

Remember, I was already in a bad place because of the red card, the suspension. So angry with myself. So angry. And then, when the team comes out and plays one of its best games of the year without me? That really knocked me on my butt.

I was like, *Should I even play in the championship?* Because, you know, the team was absolutely the most important thing to me. Winning State, that was what I wanted more than anything. So if my sitting the game out would help the team win, I would totally do that. It would kill me inside, it would break my heart, but I would totally do it.

I just wasn't sure if I should. That whole weekend, I was in agony, wondering what to do. I was going to go talk to Coach Orostieta on Monday, ask him what I should do. But in the end, it turned out to be Catalina I talked to.

Catalina Forero, center back: I saw Kaitlyn Monday morning getting off the bus. I was getting off my bus, she was getting off hers, and we were both heading into school. She looked terrible. Walking along, head down, just miserable.

Now, obviously, Kaitlyn and I weren't best friends or anything. We'd gotten off to a bad start, her coming in and taking the captain's armband like she did. That kinda put a damper on our relationship. But still, she was a teammate. And there she was, looking so awful. So I asked her what was up.

Kaitlyn Baker, central midfielder: I wasn't sure what to say to her. I was feeling like an idiot about the whole thing. You know, wondering if I was being stupid, if I was making a big deal out of nothing, if the whole thing was in my head. But of course, the whole thing *was* in my head. That was the problem. My head.

In the end, I told her. Told her all of it. Told her I wasn't sure if I should play. If the team was better without me.

Catalina Forero, center back: I was like, *Oh, man, this is not good. This is not good at all.* I told her that, too. I was like, "No, Kaitlyn. We can't have this. We can't have you thinking like this. Not now."

Because, I mean honestly, Kaitlyn Baker was the heart of that team. That team's competitive streak? Its fight? Its refusal to lose? That was Kaitlyn, pure and simple. And I told her so, right there by the buses before school. I told her we had to have her. And not this sad, miserable Kaitlyn, doubting herself. We needed fire-breathing, meat-eating, kick-you-in-the-ass-if-you-don't-play-as-hard-as-she-does Kaitlyn. That's who we needed.

And I told her that's the Kaitlyn who'd better show up for practice after school that day. The team couldn't win with this new Kaitlyn. We needed ass-kicker Kaitlyn.

Standing there by the buses, it was a little hard to tell if my speech had done any good, but after school, when we were all in the locker room getting ready for practice, it was the old Kaitlyn who showed up. Girls were still in their street clothes, still getting changed, and Kaitlyn was already barking at them. Hell, she walked in the room barking. "We got this, people! We're unstoppable!" You know how she talks. "If we give 100%, there's no way we can lose, so that *better* be what I see today! 100%!"

It was such a relief. God, can you imagine if sad, mopey Kaitlyn had showed up? We wouldn't have stood a chance.

Chamique Lennox, goalkeeper: Tough week. Very tough week. Hayley worked me like a dog.

You know Hayley kind of took over coaching me, right? She was good, too. Really seemed to enjoy it. Coach Orostieta, I barely saw him that week. He was with the rest of the team, Hayley was with me. Me and the other girl, I guess.

Coach brought this girl in to be my backup. I honestly can't remember her name. Tall girl. I think she was from the volleyball team? Basketball? Something. She never played, thank goodness. Honestly, she was sort of a "worst case scenario" kind of thing. I mean, it was bad enough they were relying on *me*. If we'd had to put *her* in, well that would basically be the apocalypse. She was, what, the fourth-string keeper? Hayley, Ruthann, me, and then Random-Volleyball-Girl-Whose-Name-I-Can't-Remember. We should have put her behind glass with a little sign that said, *Break In Case Of Emergency*. I don't remember much about her except that she was there, off to the side, watching me do drills with Hayley. She stood in the opposite goal during scrimmages. Got shelled, I'm sure.

Anyway, that's not important. What's important is Hayley working me like a dog. Non-stop drills. Dive left, dive right. Face the other direction, lie on your belly, jump up, turn around, make the save. Just these crazy drills, bang, bang, bang, bang, non-stop. It was exhausting.

And kinda fun, too, I guess. I think... You know, I think by that point, I'd gotten through the worst part. Those first couple weeks, when I'd been thrown into goal and was just getting killed, that's when I was closest to breaking. That's when I felt overwhelmed. But after surviving that, I think I came to peace with the whole thing. Started to relax. Started to accept that, *Yep, I really am the starting keeper.* And once I got to that point, I guess I could take some miserable practices without falling to pieces. I could take Hayley Swanson's non-stop drills without bursting into tears. All it took was getting my head right. Coming to peace with the whole thing.

Lisa Roney, center back: That was a very odd week of practice. In so many ways, the team should have been riding high. I mean, we'd just played this great game, we were getting ready for the championship game, so we should have been totally focused, right? Totally confident. But it was really mixed. Some people were doing great, others were really struggling.

Chamique, she was doing great. When we'd run scrimmages, I remember her seeming so much more confident. Calling out directions for us. Yelling orders. I remember this one scrimmage that week, maybe Wednesday or Thursday, there was a ball coming in, a high ball, maybe a corner or a cross or something. I was moving to get my head on it, and all of a sudden I hear Chamique coming up behind me screaming,

"Keeper! Keeper!" Just screaming it, then snatching the ball out of mid-air. It caught us all off guard, because, you know, she'd been so quiet up to that point.

Hayley Swanson was on the sideline, cheering her on. "That's how you do it, Chamique! Take control!" Actually, everyone on the team was congratulating her. It felt like a breakthrough moment, you know? She was finally acting like a starting goalkeeper. Like she deserved to be back there. And just in time, right? Championship game on Friday, we needed her at her best. Heck, we needed *everyone* at their best.

Coach Orostieta, he was doing well that week. It was his last week of practice, you know. One more game, then he was retiring. You'd think that would make him totally stressed out, but it didn't seem to. He was really cheerful all week. Happy with the team, full of optimism about the final. I don't know, maybe his attitude was, *I've only got one more week of this. I'd better enjoy it.* That's what it seemed like at least. It seemed like he'd decided to enjoy himself. Enjoy his last week as a high school coach.

Kaitlyn, she was... she was pretty good, I guess. Though I remember a few times feeling like she was a little off. Not super-off, but just a little. She'd missed the previous game, of course. The red card. And, I don't know... I think that messed her up a little. Like, she was working *extra* hard in practice, being *extra* motivated. I think she was trying to make up for the red card. She wasn't awful or anything, but just a little off.

Estefania was off, too. Her brother died that year. Did you know that? He'd died, like, the week before, I think. So that girl, she had a lot on her head, you know? And that week she was a little like Kaitlyn, in a way. Working extra hard? Maybe to forget the pain? I don't know.

I'm pretty lucky, you know? I've never had to play through something like that. If my brother had died that year, how would I have dealt with it? I have no idea. I hope I'd deal with it as well as Estefania did. She's made of pretty strong stuff.

Estefania Higuain, left back: I'm glad we made it to the final. I'm glad we had a game left. Because, the way I played in the semifinal – super distracted and out of it? – if that had been the last game of the year, I'd have been annoyed with myself the whole off-season. I mean, that's no way to end a season. You can't end your season just kind of sleep-walking around the field. You've got to give it 100%. It should be your best game of the whole year, really. If the season has to end, you want to end it with no regrets.

So that was my goal for the final. No regrets. 100% effort. From the opening whistle to the close, I was gonna go as hard as I could. I was gonna finish that game with absolutely nothing left. My gas tank completely dry.

It was partially for Hugo, but it was also partially for me. It was for both of us. When Friday came, I was

174

gonna play for both of us. And when it was all over –
win or lose – I was going to be able to say, *You know
what, Estefania, you did everything you could.   You
gave everything you had.*   And Hugo, he'd be looking
down on it, and he'd be proud of me.

So, yeah, all week in practice, that was my attitude. On
game day, that was my attitude. In the locker room
getting dressed, then getting on the bus, then riding
across town for the game, then warming up on their
field, the whole time I was thinking the same thing.
*Tonight, I'm giving absolutely everything. 100%. Win
or lose, I'm going to play a game I can be proud of.*

C.I. DeMann

State Championship Game

Martha Sullivan, West Sycamore: The game was at home, of course, since we were the higher seed. It's funny what a switch that was. At the beginning of the year, you think anyone would have predicted us being the favorites and East being the team that just barely snuck into the playoffs? Nobody would've predicted that. Nobody. And yet, that's how it played out. Insane.

So yeah, it was a home game, and we actually had a bit of a crowd. They'd mentioned it on the morning announcements a few times that week. *Come support our girls this Friday as they play for the state title!* Something like that. The football team, they'd lost, their season was done, so we didn't have to compete with them for the spotlight. Plus, we were gonna play on their field, with the big bleachers and the PA system and the press box and all that. That was exciting.

Getting dressed in the locker room beforehand – it was our normal locker room, by the way. Not up at the football stadium. We got dressed, then walked up there in our uniforms, bags over our shoulders. But anyway, the locker room was pretty quiet. Destinee was giving us her usual pep talks, I'm sure. Coach probably said something, but I can't remember what. I was pretty focused on myself, thinking about what I had to do.

Moments like that, they're fun. The nervousness, the worry, the butterflies, I think I sort of like them. Some people probably hate it, but for me, that was part of the fun of that night. The nervousness in the locker room. The butterflies walking out to the field. The heart racing from seeing the big crowd, hearing their cheers when we showed up.

Like I said, I'll bet some people hate all those feelings, but I really liked them. It made the whole thing more fun for me.

Catalina Forero, East Sycamore: It was our second trip to West that year. The first game, there'd probably been 20 people in the stands. This time, it was probably 500. Maybe more. It's hard to tell, since the first game was at some small field with these little tiny bleachers, but for the championship, they'd moved us to the football field, with these big giant stands. To be honest, it was probably a lot more than 500. A thousand? It was a good crowd.

I remember, during warm ups I saw Hayley talking with Maria Solana. How much they could talk, I'm not sure. I guess Hayley spoke a little Spanish. Anyway, I just remember thinking how funny it was. Our best player, their best player, and neither one of them playing. They're over there in street clothes, shaking hands, hanging out. It was funny to me in the moment. It's funny to me now, even. Two of the best players in the world, and they didn't even get to play.

Maria Solana, West Sycamore: We could not say a lot. My English was still not very good and her Spanish was also not very good, but I still think it was very nice of her to come say hello. Hayley is a good person. I have heard people say that she is a little scary, but I think that is just because she is so tall and strong and confident. I think all goalkeepers are like that, but when you are as good as Hayley Swanson, maybe it is even more so. But, no, she is not scary. She is very nice.

We were standing there watching the warm ups and talking a little. I remember it being cold. It was a very big crowd, because we were in the big stadium, the football stadium. American football, that is. My family was there, and Hayley's family was there. I think I could probably ask her that in English. *Your family? Here?* That sort of thing. Very simple.

After a few minutes, Hayley and I said goodbye and went to be with our teams. Everyone was very excited, very nervous. I wish I could have played. It was an exciting game.

Carlos Orostieta, East Sycamore: Oh, what a game, what a game. Such a way to go out! You were there? Oh, you missed a good one, my friend.

I would not say it was our best game, when you speak of performance. We certainly didn't play as well as in the semi-final. And not even as well as the first time we played West Sycamore, back in the regular season. But what the game lacked in beauty, it more than made up for in drama. So much drama! I will never forget it. No one will.

Clementine Thiamale, West Sycamore: The game started slowly, as I recall. Maybe people were a little nervous, afraid to mess up on the big stage. I know I was, just a little. I played very safe those first few minutes. Safe passes, nothing too difficult. And, of course, that was how Susan Douglas wanted to play all the time. Safe and easy. It's funny, all season long, Coach Nolan told us, *First tackle, first foul, first shot, first goal.* Then when we finally made it to the championship game, all that was out the window and we were playing things very, very safe. I find that sort of ironic.

We were in the football stadium, you know. Big crowd. I could see Curtis in the stands, sitting with my family. They hadn't come to the game together, but they saw each other while they were looking for seats and decided to sit together. When I saw that, I was like, *Oh, dear. Papa's going to embarrass me, isn't he?*

[laughs] But Curtis said it was fine. He said he and Papa mostly just talked about the game. He could only understand about half of what my papa said, so he just sort of nodded and smiled. So funny.

Anyway, the game started slow.

Kaitlyn Baker, East Sycamore: It was a very different game from the first time we played, back in the regular season. They had this new girl in the middle, and she was really frustrating. Dribble, dribble, dribble, short pass here, short pass there, dribble, dribble, dribble. That's how Susan played. I was trying to dispossess her but couldn't. Susan was pretty amazing with the ball. Her teammates were doing well with it, too. Destinee Jones, she's quality. Clementine Thiamale, also a really good player. That little striker of theirs, I can't remember her name, but she was quality, too.

So that's how I remember the game starting; being frustrated. Chasing the ball a lot. That's really annoying. It gets you frustrated, and you start taking chances, start losing your defensive shape. If the other team's any good, they'll punish you for that. Which is what happened, of course.

I think it was the 15th minute or so. We'd had a tiny bit of possession, but not much. Any time we'd get the ball, whether it was me or Vilma Aguilar or whoever, we'd be so excited, we'd want to push, push, push. Because, you know, when were we gonna get the ball again?

So it was the 15th minute. One of us got the ball back, and the whole team kind of surged forward, trying to make something happen. And of course, that left room behind us, which they took advantage of.

Nykesha Nolan, West Sycamore: It was a beautiful counter attack. East got the ball and went screaming forward, trying to make something happen. I can't remember who took it from them. Clementine, probably. Stole the ball, blew someone up. Typical Clementine.

Carlos Orostieta, East Sycamore: Their defensive midfielder, the African girl, what was her name? Thiamale? Yes, that's it. She started their counter. Took the ball off Vilma Aguilar, I think it was. A very physical player, Thiamale. Always pushed the limits of what a foul was. I would have loved to coach her. Players like that, they drive you crazy when they're on the other team, but of course, you wish you had someone just like them.

So Thiamale stole the ball, and immediately West was off and running. Such an offense they had. And that was without Solana! Can you imagine if she'd been playing?

So they were racing down the field, two of them. Thiamale and Jones, I believe it was. No, Douglas and Jones. Yes. Douglas and Jones. A couple quick touches, back and forth, sprinting the whole time. Such a strong counter-attack. Their coach, Nykesha Nolan, she was young and inexperienced, but she knew her team's strengths. She let them run.

They came racing down the field, very fast, just a few passes, and, boom, boom, boom, it was 1-0.

Nykesha Nolan, West Sycamore: It was Jones who scored it. Susan laid it off to her in the box, and Destinee one-timed it in. A nice hard shot, too. Jones had a good right leg. She could really pop it.

Man, oh man, did that goal give our girls a shot in the arm. They were going crazy. All of us were, even me on the sideline. Maria Solana was next to me, and I remember hugging her really hard, then stopping myself, worried I might hurt her leg.

Out on the field, Destinee was so pumped. You know how she was. Just screaming, laughing, bringing the whole team in for a big hug. Destinee really was the heart of that team. Great captain. Great kid.

Destinee Jones, West Sycamore: I was going nuts. Celebrated with the team, of course – big giant group of us – but I was also looking over at my family in the stands. Dad there, all my brothers, and I scored! How friggin' great was that? They were up in the bleachers, all bundled up. It was cold, so you could see everyone's breath like this big cloud of steam. My dad was standing up, cheering. My brothers, they started yelling my name. You know, chanting it. "De-sti-nee! De-sti-nee!" It was so great.

Scoring that goal in front of them, I really needed that. I needed them to see that soccer was cool, that soccer was fun. And banging in that early goal, I think it helped me the rest of the game. I knew I'd won them over.

I kept looking up there, the whole rest of the game. I'd see them up there in the stands, freezing their tails off, and I'd be like, *Yeah, they're behind me. The whole family's behind me.* It helped. It really did.

Catalina Forero, East Sycamore: I was so pissed. Soooooooooo pissed. That first goal? Totally my fault. I was running the defense, it was me telling the back line to move forward. So, yeah, I'll take the blame for them getting behind us. That never should have happened. We were better than that.

I remember they were celebrating, mobbing each other, hugging, all that stuff. Kaitlyn pulled us in for a little pep talk. She was like, "This ain't over. There's still a lot of soccer to be played. A lot of soccer."

And, truth is, looking around that circle of girls, I didn't see much fear. Yeah, people were upset, but nobody looked like they were ready to give up. Even Chamique. She was upset, sure. But devastated? No. She'd been in goal a few games now. She was getting some confidence.

So even though I was pissed about the goal, pissed about my mistakes, I wasn't pissed about how the team responded. All around that circle, the attitude was great. There was no giving up. Everyone was like, *We ain't going out like this. Let's go win this thing.*

Carlos Orostieta, East Sycamore: If I can tell you the truth, I think it was a good thing, giving up that early goal. I believe it woke my girls up, put some steel in their spine. Roney and Forero, especially. They'd been overrun by that counter, and they knew it. You could see it in their eyes.

Chamique Lennox, East Sycamore: Oh yeah, it was game on from that point. Everyone got deadly serious. Kaitlyn, deadly serious. Catalina, deadly serious. Hell, even Lisa, who usually wasn't all aggro like that, now she was all business. It was kind of cool, to be honest. I was back there in goal thinking, *Man, this is the real deal. This is for the title.*

That's a little weird, isn't it? Up to then, I'd been trying to stay calm, not get stressed. I was kinda like, *Oh, just another game. I just wanna play well.* But giving up that early goal, that flipped a switch, and I was like, *No, this is the biggest game in the world right now.*

It was kind of fun, to be honest. Playing in a big, big game, with everything on the line, it's stressful, sure, but it's also kind of fun.

Estefania Higuain, East Sycamore: We did much better from there. Turned up the pressure, kept them from playing keep-away, held the ball a little more, moved it down to their end a little, got a few offensive chances, a few shots. Just all-around better.

Their winger, she was slow. I figured out pretty early that I could get behind her, so we were working the left side a lot. I was getting forward, sending a bunch of crosses in, trying to make something happen. I remember, I nearly had an assist on one cross. It was a nice one. I really got my foot on it, put it right there where Gloria could get her head on it. That's Gloria Cayetano, our striker. I put it right on her head, maybe in the... 30th minute? She put it wide, but it was still a good chance. We had a number of good chances.

That whole game, I was thinking about Hugo a lot. Like, maybe I'd be feeling tired, maybe I'd be catching my breath or something, and I'd think, *No. Get it in gear. For Hugo.* I wasn't gonna let him down. I wasn't gonna have two straight bad games.

Martha Sullivan, West Sycamore: It was cold as hell. That's one of my main memories of that night, how cold it was, how windy. I remember my short sleeves were okay at the beginning of the game, but at some point in the first half I was wishing I'd worn my long sleeve undershirt. I was running around a lot, trying to stay warm, but it was like a cold front moved in or something.

One of East's center backs commented on it. I can't remember which one, but there was a pause, maybe for a throw-in or something, and she said to me, "Dang, is it getting colder?" She was beating on her arms, trying to stay warm.

Well, anyway... what was the next big thing? I guess it was the free kick. When was that? 30th minute? 35th?

It started with a foul, I guess, but I don't remember that. I just remember it was maybe 25 yards from goal, pretty much center of the pitch. Dangerous spot. It was East's captain who took the kick. Kaitlyn Baker. Damn, it was a nice kick, too. We'd set up a wall. The tall girls, that is. Not me. But the big girls, they got everything set just right, had a nice tight wall, and it didn't make any difference. Baker put it right over us, curled it into that top corner. Hell of a kick, hell of a goal.

Carlos Orostieta, East Sycamore: Oh, my goodness, such a free kick! You should have seen it, my friend. Kaitlyn Baker, she curled it just over their wall, then just under the crossbar. Such a shot! Their goalkeeper, she had no chance. She got a good jump on it, too. As soon as it popped up over the wall, she saw it, started tracking it, moving sideways. She looked good, but it didn't matter. Shots like that, they're unstoppable, aren't they? Perfect curl, way up in the top corner. I don't believe any keeper is stopping that shot. Not her, not Chamique Lennox, not even Hayley Swanson. It was a perfect kick.

Kaitlyn Baker, East Sycamore: I'm not gonna lie, it felt pretty good.

You know, you practice those all the time, right? Bending them over the wall like that? And yeah, sure, you hit a few. But that's practice. Hitting one in a game? I'd never done it. And I haven't really done it since. Not like that. So it felt pretty great.

And it was good for the team, too. A big confidence boost for all of us. The referee blew the whistle for halftime not long after that, and we were all feeling pretty good. West had been the better team at the start, but we'd owned the last, what, 20, 25 minutes? The momentum had completely shifted.

So, at halftime, we were feeling good. Tie score? All the momentum? We thought we had the game in hand.

Susan Douglas, West Sycamore: At halftime, we were under our little tent, down behind one of the goals. I don't know what happened that night – cold front or something – but it got super-cold over the course of the game. We'd started the game wearing our normal uniforms – shorts, shirts – and then at halftime, we were all scrambling to put on extra layers. Some of the bench girls were holding up towels so people couldn't see us changing. It was crazy how cold it got. There was a breeze, too. It was pretty awful, by the end.

I remember being jealous, because some of the girls had nice long sleeve undershirts. You know, fancy expensive stuff. Nike. Under Armour. Whatever. All I had was the t-shirt I'd worn to school that day. I put it on, of course. I needed something.

Aside from all that, the main thing I remember from halftime was seeing the Galtons, my foster parents. I'll never forget it. We were all there together, people are changing, coach is giving pep talks. Destinee, too. Oh, and I remember Maria was talking to me. Giving me advice and stuff. Through an interpreter. Anyway, at some point, I looked over at that big crowd we had, just checking it out, and I saw the Galtons sitting there, all bundled up.

Completely blew my mind. Absolutely floored me.

I mean, yeah, of course they'd known about the game, but... I guess when you've bounced around foster care for awhile, you just get used to people not caring. Or not caring beyond the bare minimum. That's what you expect, the bare minimum. You don't expect anything beyond that. And you certainly don't expect them to, you know, *care*. To act like proud parents. Or grandparents, in this case. But there they were, up in the crowd with everyone else's families.

I actually remember getting kind of flustered about the whole thing. I think my face probably went bright red. Maria was still trying to talk to me, but I was a million miles away, not hearing a word. I was just thinking, you know, *I've got family here, just like everyone else.*

It might seem like the smallest thing in the world, but to me it was huge.

Lisa Roney, East Sycamore: Halftime was down at one end of the field. We were all bundled up against the cold. People changing, putting on extra layers.

Spirits were pretty high, actually. Tie game. All the

momentum with us. We were feeling good.

As usual, the defense was sitting together. Catalina was talking the most. Her and Hayley. They were like, "No more goals. None. We're shutting them out from here on." That sort of thing. "No more falling for that rope-a-dope crap. Let 'em play keep-away all they want, we're not falling for it." That sort of thing.

I remember Hayley talking with Chamique about that goal she gave up. Building up her confidence, telling her it was no big deal. Hayley did a good job with her. She's gonna make a good coach someday.

Oh, here's a funny memory; I told you that people were changing into warmer clothes. Well, I remember I'd just done that, just put on an undershirt, and when I came out from behind all the coats and towels and stuff that everyone was holding up, I saw these two little boys coming over. They were, like, nine years old. Ten, maybe. Cute. So they're running up toward the tent. I see them coming, so I call out to them. "Sorry, boys, you can't come over here. People are changing." Something like that.

They stopped, of course. They're maybe, I don't know, 20 feet away. The older one, he yells, "Chamique's our cousin." I knew Chamique had cousins, but I'd never met them. I say, "Sorry, but you can't come over. I'll tell her you said hi."

Well, they start whispering to each other, and then the older one yells over to me, "Hey, you're Lisa, aren't you?" And I'm like, "Yeah." And they start giggling, and say, "Are you Chamique's *girlfriend*?" And I'm suddenly like, *Oh, hell, how do I answer this?* Because, you know, Chamique, she'd come out, of course, but it was still pretty new. And I'm looking at these boys, wondering what they know, what they don't know, and finally, I'm like, "Yeaaaah." And then they turn and run off, giggling and laughing. And I remember thinking to myself, *I have no idea how that just went.* I really couldn't tell, were they laughing *at* me or *with* me? Or maybe they were just being silly little boys laughing at the idea of their cousin dating someone, anyone.

I guess that's not exactly a funny story, is it? More of a confusing story. But that's typical of being a gay teenager. You're never entirely sure where things stand. Never sure what people think of you. It just so happens that this confusing little thing happened at halftime of the state championship.

I'm glad Chamique didn't see them. I didn't even tell her they came by. She had enough to think about. She needed to stay focused.

Maria Solana, West Sycamore: During halftime, I was trying to talk to Susan Douglas, but it was hard. I had to use translators, of course. Yoreli or Daniela probably. But they had things they needed to think about. Coach Nolan was giving them advice, giving them orders, and they wanted to listen to that. Plus, everyone was putting on warmer clothes. It got very cold that game. I think we started the game in autumn, and we finished it in winter.

So everybody was very distracted with all of those things, and there I was in the middle of it, trying to find someone to translate for me so I could talk to Susan. And then Susan didn't even seem like she wanted to listen. She was looking into the stands, looking at her family, I suppose. She was distracted, the Latina girls were distracted. Everyone had something to do except me. I was just there in the middle of it all with nothing to do. I wanted to help my team, but I couldn't.

Finally, I decided that maybe I should just be quiet. Step back. It was a terrible feeling. I know there is a word in English for when you aren't needed. When you are just in the way. I can't think of it, but that is how I felt at halftime that day. Like the team didn't need me. Like I was in the way. It was a very sad feeling.

Chamique Lennox, East Sycamore: I spent most of halftime talking with Hayley. Breaking down that first goal. What I'd done, what I could've done differently. Getting ready for the second half.

To be honest, I was in a pretty good place. It was, what, my 5th game in goal? A lot of the fear was gone.

I remember this funny moment where I told Hayley I felt really bad for the other team's keeper. I was like, "Did you see her on Kaitlyn's goal? I don't think she could have played that any better. You think she could have played that better?" I was genuinely feeling bad for the girl.

And then Hayley was like, "Are you kidding me right now? Hell with that girl! This is war, Chamique!"

It's funny now, but at the time it was a little scary. I was like, *Oops, I probably shouldn't have said that out loud.* Hayley was much more competitive than me, which I'm sure is part of the reason she's playing in World Cups and I'm not.

Well, whatever. I did feel sorry for their keeper. She was a nice girl. Michelle, her name was. We had a big hug after the game. She was nice.

Carlos Orostieta, East Sycamore: And then it was time for the second half. And let me tell you, that was as difficult a half as I have ever been a part of. So much drama, so much difficulty.

It did not start well, I can tell you that. It did not start well at all.

Estefania Higuain, East Sycamore: I don't even know how to describe it. It was almost like... it was like we'd switched places. You know, East Sycamore, we were supposed to be the big time program, with all the state titles, all the future national teamers. West? They were supposed to be the underdogs.

But in that second half? No, it was just the opposite. They came out of halftime playing *great.* They had all the energy, all the movement. Every pass was right on target. Every possession had us scrambling backwards, desperately guarding goal. It was terrible.

How many shots did we give up in the first ten minutes? Two? Three? It was just bang, bang, bang, right from the start. Chamique, she really came up big for us.

I remember this one play, West had a corner kick. As we were setting up in the box, Catalina was just beside herself. She was like, "What the hell's going on, guys? We're better than this! Get your heads out of your butts!"

Normally, it was Kaitlyn yelling stuff like that, but now it was Catalina, too. Hell, I was ready to start yelling. Yelling at myself, at least.

It was bad. After ten, fifteen minutes of getting our butts kicked, I was really starting to think we were done for. I was wondering if West was just the better team. If they deserved the title, not us.

Susan Douglas, West Sycamore: I'm not sure why, but we really came out flying. East... I think maybe East was thinking a little too much or something. Remember that first goal? When they let their back four get a little too far forward? I think maybe they were over-reacting to that. Like, overcompensating. Keeping their back four *too* far back. Locking things down a little *too* tight, you know?

I'm not sure. All I know is there was a ton of room to work with and we took it. We moved forward.

Destinee was flying up that left side, Deavon and Yoreli were flying up the right. Daniela looked good in the middle, banging with their center backs.

And Martha Sullivan? She was on fire. Just pouring shots on goal. Didn't she hit one off the post? I think she did. And I think another shot was saved. Yeah, I remember it now, it was just *barely* saved. How Martha didn't get a goal in those first few minutes, I have no idea. She could've had two or three.

It was funny, playing with Martha. She had this funny way of playing. She was a really small girl, really petite. But as a striker, playing in there with all those big, giant center backs, she had to be really sneaky. Sort of hang out in their blind spots. Stay just outside their field of vision. Make herself invisible, I guess.

So anytime I got the ball, I was almost afraid to look at her. *[laughs]* Because, you know, if I look directly at her, the center backs will see where I'm looking, and Martha won't be invisible anymore, right? That's how it felt to me, anyway. So when I was out there with the ball, I tried to look everywhere *except* at Martha. I'm looking left, looking right, only seeing Martha out the corner of my eye, you know? It was a funny situation. You should ask Maria Solana about that. Ask her if she did the same thing. Of course, with Maria, she can probably look wherever the hell she wants. The defense won't be able to stop her anyway.

So, that's how the second half started. We were killing them. Really had them on the ropes.

Kaitlyn Baker, East Sycamore: But they never scored. Shot after shot after shot and they never scored. And at a certain point, we started to notice. We were like, *Hey, it's still tied. We're surviving.* That gave us some confidence.

Eventually – maybe the 55th minute or so – we finally got a little breakout. West was still pushing, pushing, pushing. Still *almost* scoring but not quite. One of their girls took a shot – probably that little striker of theirs – and Chamique got hold of it. She picked her head up...

[pauses]

You know, Chamique really grew a lot over those playoffs. Picking her head up like that? Looking up the field for runners? She wouldn't have done that a few weeks earlier. She was growing. She was getting better.

So anyway, she grabs the ball, looks up, and sees me with a bunch of room to run into. Gives me a quick little throw and, hey, what do you know? We've got a counterattack!

Over on my right side, I guess that would've been Ye-Jee Park. On my left was Mary Ogwumike. No, it was Gloria. Gloria Cayetano. So the three of us are hauling ass upfield. West's defense, I think the only girls in front of us were their two center backs, so we've got us a nice little 3-on-2. The crowd sees it – big crowd that night, of course – the crowd sees it and starts going crazy. I pass it over to Ye-Jee, hit her in stride, she passes it back to me. We're still running, their center backs are still scrambling back. I pass it over to Gloria on the left, she's got a good look at goal, and West's center back absolutely takes her out. Just clobbers her. Gloria's down, ball's skittering out of bounds, ref's blowing his whistle for a foul.

I was furious. I immediately started laying into the ref. I was like, "You gotta card her! You *gotta* card her!" He's pretty much ignoring me. He's like, "Free kick. No yellow." I'm beside myself. Gloria's down on the ground, seeing stars, and I'm like, "You have *got* to be kidding me! How is that not a yellow? Hell, it could be a damn red!" The ref, he couldn't care less what I have to say, he's just got the ball sitting there for a free kick and starts pacing out ten steps.

Well, once again, I was an idiot. I know this. I admit it freely. But I was just so damn angry. I looked down, saw the ball sitting there for the free kick, and I wound up and kicked it as hard as I could. Didn't even look. Just kicked it.

And, of course, what happens? It hits one of the West girls, right in the shoulder. Just my luck.

Well, no surprise, she's angry. I don't actually know who it was I hit, but she was pissed.

Destinee Jones, West Sycamore: It was Connie Valenzuela, our left back. I think the ball hit her

shoulder, then hit her ear. Hurt like hell, she told me.
She was *furious*.

Kaitlyn Baker, East Sycamore: She turns and comes
at me. Hell, the whole team came at me. The girl
shoves me, I shove back. The other players are getting
involved. Someone gets me from behind, starts pulling
me away, other players are diving in, getting in faces,
yelling. It was a total disaster. I didn't even see the
whole fight, really. It's hard to, when you're in the
middle of it. Middle of this big clot of people,
everyone yelling and shoving each other.

Eventually, everyone gets separated. Calmed down.
Ref gives out, like, five or six yellow cards. I was like,
"Oh, *now* he pulls out his card! Where was that
earlier?" I'm surprised he didn't give me a second
yellow and toss me out of the game. I was an idiot.

So things calmed down. I apologized to the girl. She
mostly accepted it. We were both still angry, of course,
but, you know, there was a game to be played. A
championship game.

It wasn't my finest moment, that's for sure. But, you
know, I was a kid. We weren't playing well, I was
frustrated, and next thing you know, there's a hockey
brawl breaking out in the middle of the field.

Martha Sullivan, West Sycamore: I avoided the
whole fight, pretty much. Stayed on the perimeter of it,
pretended I was all angry, maybe yelled a few things. I
saw this East Sycamore girl who was kind of doing the

same as me. You know, she didn't *really* want to go into the middle of it, but was kind of pretending she wanted to, just to put on a good face. We saw each other and could tell. We grabbed each other's jerseys to keep the other from going into the big mob of girls, even though we both knew neither of us wanted to go in. It's hilarious, just thinking about it. Two non-fighters pretending they're keeping each other from fighting. Hilarious.

I actually look for that now. If I'm watching sports on TV and a fight breaks out, I immediately start looking around the perimeter of the fight for those two people who clearly don't want to fight but are kind of jointly pretending they do. It's so funny. Every fight's got a few of us.

Destinee Jones, West Sycamore: So that whole thing took about three or four minutes, I guess. Ref cleared everyone out, and East took their free kick. Didn't do much with it.

We were still playing well. Susan Douglas, especially. Martha Sullivan, too. Great game for both of them, especially in that second half. But it wasn't either of them who got our next goal. It was like the least likely person ever. Someone who I honestly don't think had ever scored a goal for us. Ever.

It was somewhere around the 65th minute. Started with me. I had the ball pretty far forward. Way out on the left, almost touching the sideline, really. Constanza ran past me, heading for the left corner. I remember I almost passed it to her, thinking we could do a little give-and-go. Me to Connie, then back to me cutting for goal. So I almost made that pass, but then I saw Martha in the middle, sneaking around like she always did, finding some open space. I saw her coming open and thought, *Damn, if I can put it right at her feet, she can re-direct it into goal.* So that's what I was trying to do, hit it low and hard, right on her foot.

Well, honestly, I couldn't have hit it much worse. Completely skied it, right over her, right over the center backs, right over the whole box and into the opposite corner. Fortunately, Susan Douglas was over there, and the ball fell right to her foot. She picked her head up, surveyed things, and sent the ball back in.

Soon as she hit it – I was over on the opposite side, remember – soon as she hit it, I was like, *Nope, way off target. Bad pass.* Because it wasn't going anywhere near either Martha or Daniela. It was heading more towards the top of the box, where no one was.

And that's when I saw Clementine racing forward like a bat out of hell. *[laughs]* It's so funny, thinking about it, because, honestly, Clementine pretty much never came forward. Not *that* far forward, at least. But there she was, barreling forward, completely alone. And here comes Susan's cross, heading right toward Clementine, and I'm like, *You've gotta be kidding me. Is Clem gonna get to that?*

So here comes Clem, here comes the ball, and I can see, no, the pass is way too high. Maybe I could have gotten to it, maybe Maria could've gotten to it, but Clementine? She was, what, five foot two? At the most? *Way* too short. No way is she getting to that pass.

But she's running, just sprinting, and then she jumps, rises, rises, gets every inch of herself into that jump, stretches herself completely out and, whatta ya know? She heads it into goal!

Well, oh my God, did we freak out. You gotta realize, people loved Clementine. She was probably everyone's favorite player on the team. Yeah, sure, I was captain. People liked me. But people *loved* Clementine. Little short girl out there blowing people up, always hustling, always smiling? We loved her. And now she scores her first goal ever? In the championship game? We lost our damn minds.

Clementine Thiamale, West Sycamore: It was pretty amazing. I just barely got my head to it. I don't think I've ever jumped that high, not before or since. But I got it. Just enough to sneak it under the crossbar.

Oh, I was so happy. *So* happy. The team was all around me, smiling, laughing, hugging me. It was wonderful. I don't think I've ever smiled so wide. Destinee Jones – you know how she is – she was laughing and dancing and making it a party. We were all over in the corner in this big mob. I think everyone was there. I even think Michelle was there. I think she ran all the way up from her goal. Oh, what a moment!

I remember at a certain point I looked into the stands and saw my family. Curtis was with them, of course, and they were all standing and cheering and going crazy. I saw my father kiss my mother, saw my mother wiping her eyes, everyone just so happy. And Curtis, I waved at him, and he waved back, smiling so wide. It was a wonderful moment. My heart is racing just thinking about it.

Nykesha Nolan, West Sycamore: So that put us up 2-1. I think there were about 15 minutes left. Maybe 20. All we had to do was finish it off and we'd be state champions. It was amazing. This nobody team from this nobody school and here we were, beating the best program in the state. Crazy. If we could hold on for a few more minutes, the trophy was ours.

Unfortunately, East knew the situation, too, and Lord almighty, did they turn up the heat. Just pinned their ears back and came at us with everything they had. I gotta be honest, those last 20 minutes were brutal. After 20 minutes of attack, attack, attack, we were suddenly defend, defend, defend. Not what we were used to, but what choice was there?

Chamique Lennox, East Sycamore: The end of the game was kind of miserable. For me, at least. One, I'd just given up that goal, so I was angry about that, and two, I didn't have anything to do. I was just standing there in front of goal watching us attack way down at the other end of the field. And it was hella cold, so I was beating on my arms, bouncing up and down, doing anything I could to stay warm, to stay ready.

The rest of the team was pressed forward, of course. I guess Catalina and Lisa were hanging back a tiny bit – you know, last line of defense – but our fullbacks? Way upfield. Our defensive midfielders? Way upfield. There was no choice, really. We were desperate. And the longer we went without scoring, the more desperate it got. Twenty minutes left. Fifteen minutes left. Ten minutes left. Five minutes left. It was awful.

Carlos Orostieta, East Sycamore: Such a push we gave them! Forward, forward, always forward! Kaitlyn Baker led the way. She was always active, of course, always energetic, always vocal, but those last 20 minutes? Oh, my, she was a house on fire. Pushing, pushing, pushing. A ball goes out of bounds? She's racing over to throw it in. It goes out for West? Kaitlyn's yelling at them to hurry up, to quit wasting time. She was on the referee, telling him to watch the time wasting.

I remember this one play, oh, it was funny. We had missed a shot – I'm not sure who it was. Cayetano. Park. It doesn't matter. And the West goalkeeper, she was taking her time putting the ball back into play. You know, just moving slowly. Adjusting the ball on the ground. Adjusting it again. Moving it to a different spot. *[laughs]* Just trying to burn as much clock as she could, you know. We all do it.

So Kaitlyn Baker, she starts counting out loud. "One, two, three, four!" Very loud, she's counting, all the way up. Then when she hit 10, she starts yelling at the referee, "Pull your card! Pull your card!" *[laughs]* I swear, Kaitlyn Baker! Such a fighter! I'm surprised the ref didn't card *her*. But he watched their keeper the rest of the game, I can tell you that.

Lisa Roney, East Sycamore: The good news is that West really wasn't attacking at all anymore. They were working so hard on defense that as soon as they'd get the ball, they'd just clear it out of there. Kick it as deep as they could. Catalina and I were back there collecting the ball, sending it forward again. Not a lot to do except watch.

That's not true, we did come forward for corner kicks. I think there was one corner that Catalina actually put on goal. Yeah, it was a good chance, as I recall. Ye-Jee took our corners, and she put one right on Catalina's head. Cat put it on goal, but their goalie knocked it away.

Their keeper had a hell of a game for them. I can't think what her name was. Washington? Jefferson? Roosevelt? *[laughs]* I'm just gonna go through all the presidents until I get it. *[laughs]* Anyway, she was good. Tall. Good hands. Not as good as Hayley Swanson, of course, but as good as Chamique? Probably.

So, yeah, we were in the box for a few corner kicks. And really, the more time passed without a goal, the farther up me and Cat went. It was crazy. So damn tense. Just awful.

C.I. DeMann

Martha Sullivan, West Sycamore: You have no idea. The defending, it was just non-stop.

And, me, I couldn't really do much to help. My job was to stay out there at midfield, out by their center backs. Just to keep them honest. Just to give us the *possibility* of a counterattack. Keep them thinking about that. Otherwise, they'd just send everyone forward, right? Keep no one back on D.

So that's what I was doing for those last twenty minutes. Hanging out at midfield, hoping someone might send a long pass my way, something I could get behind their center backs with. It never happened, though. Their center backs were really good. I mean, of course they were good. It was Forero and Roney. They've played in World Cups.

But anyway, that was me. Hanging out at midfield, praying for the clock to tick faster. It was pretty miserable, to be honest.

Nykesha Nolan, West Sycamore: So we made it to the end of regular time. How many minutes of stoppage time were there? Four minutes? Five? I remember it seemed like a lot, but whatever. Let's call it five minutes. I think they probably had five or six corner kicks in those five minutes. That sounds like an exaggeration, but I swear it's true. Five or six corners. Two or three shots on goal. It was non-stop pressure.

It's tough being a coach in moments like that. You'd much rather be a player. Because, as a coach, there's nothing you can do. You want to run out on the field and help your girls, but you can't. And yelling from the sideline only helps so much. Mostly what you do is watch, just like everyone else. Watch, pray, cross all your fingers and toes. It's nerve-wracking.

So anyway, at a certain point, I'm thinking, *Stoppage time's got to be over by now.* So I'm yelling at the ref, "Blow your whistle, blow your whistle!" He's ignoring me. As he should. I'm yelling anyway. What else can I do?

Kaitlyn Baker, East Sycamore: You don't know what desperation is until you've been in a situation like that. I mean, *any* game where you're down a goal in stoppage time is desperate. But in the state championship? I was losing my mind.

We had plenty of chances, I'll say that much. Corner kick, defender heads it over the end line. Another corner kick, keeper punches it out the side. Throw in, shot on goal, someone blocks it over the end line. It went like that over and over and over. And each time, I'm hustling to get the ball in as fast as possible. I'm yelling at the ball girl to give us a spare ball. I'm yelling at Ye-Jee to run to the corner, get the kick in. I'm running over to the side line to do the throw in myself. I was just going out of my mind. It was unbelievably tense.

Maria Solana, West Sycamore: You start to wonder, *When is he going to blow the whistle? It must be time! It must be!* I was standing with Coach Nolan and she was yelling those things at the referee. I was not. I was silent, just watching it all. It was a terrible time. East had so many good chances. So many corners. So many shots. Michelle Washington, she did a wonderful job in goal.

On the last corner kick – I am certain it was the last kick. Everyone was sure he would blow the whistle after it – on the last corner, East had all their players forward. All of them, even their goalkeeper. Nobody was back on defense. Tall girls, short girls, everyone was in the box, trying to score a goal. And, of course, all our girls were there, too, trying to defend. It was such a sight to see.

The game's last kick and all I could do was watch from the side. That was a terrible feeling. So helpless.

Catalina Forero, East Sycamore: I remember so much from that final kick. Like it was yesterday.

I remember it being cold as hell. Big clouds of steam everywhere. I remember the penalty box being super-crowded. I remember Chamique being right there next to me with her keeper's uniform, her big, giant keeper gloves. I remember telling her, "Don't use your hands." Anytime I see a keeper come forward like that, I always wonder if they're gonna forget where they are and accidentally grab the ball.

So me and Lisa and Chamique were all there in the middle. All the tall girls. West had some decent-sized girls, too. We were all bodied up to each other. My girl was leaning on me, I was leaning on her. It was super-tense. I think everyone knew this was the last kick of the game.

So Ye-Jee sent the ball in. I remember it like it was super-slow motion. At first, I was thinking I had a shot at it, then I realized it was going over my head, so I start backing up. My girl's fighting me. I spin, trying to get behind her, but it was a friggin' mess in there. Just super-crowded.

We're all trying to judge where the ball's going. It's going well past me. Chamique and Lisa are back there, and they're fighting to get in position. West's goalie's coming out, fighting through people, trying to punch it away.

Lisa told me afterward that she nearly got her head to it, but I didn't actually see. All I saw was West's goalie rising up to punch the ball and missing. All those big tall girls in there, all those people trying to get their head on it, and what happens? Everyone misses, including the keeper. The ball falls to the ground, and who's standing there? Estefania.

Estefania Higuain, East Sycamore: I couldn't believe it. I was way back at the far post. All the tall girls were in the middle, but Ye-Jee's ball went past all of them. Not *way* past them. Just barely past them, really. But they all missed it, including West's keeper, who missed her punch.

And then I'm looking down at my feet, and the ball's

there. All I had to do was poke it into the net. Easiest goal anyone's ever scored.

[pauses, shakes head]

I don't know if you've ever scored a last-second goal like that, but it's crazy. Your brain just kind of turns off. I mean, if someone were to ask me, "How would you want to celebrate a big goal?" I'd probably say, I don't know, "Grab my teammates in a hug," or something like that. Something sensible. But when it actually happens, there's no thinking. Your brain just turns off and you run. You just run. Where? Wherever. You don't know. Your legs just go wherever they want to go. I ran toward the far corner – screaming, I guess – then turned and ran back toward midfield. I think that's about when the rest of the team caught up with me. It was probably Kaitlyn who caught me. I think it was her who grabbed me and pulled me into a big hug, and then the rest of the team was there, too, all of us freaking out.

My brain kind of came back then. Everyone was hugging me. Screaming. We were near midfield, going crazy, and I could see the sideline, and everyone there was going crazy, too. The bench players were grabbing each other, jumping up and down, screaming. Coach Orostieta, I think he had a fist up in the air or something.

The whole thing was kind of unreal. Or is the word surreal? I don't know, I just know I'll never forget it. Ever. That was the only last-second goal I've ever scored. Have you had a play like that? No? Probably most people never do. I'm glad I did. It was amazing. Like I said, your brain just completely turns off. Reality disappears for a minute or so, and when you come back, you're in a totally different place on the field, and you're not sure how you got there. It's crazy. There's nothing like it.

Nykesha Nolan, West Sycamore: And that was that. Tie game. Absolute last play of the game. Very last kick. Just heartbreaking.

I don't know which one of them actually scored it. A center back, I think. It was such a mob scene in there, I barely saw what happened. Kick goes in, everyone's going for it, it falls to the ground, someone's there, and the ball's in the net.

Over on the sideline, we just deflated. On the field, too. The East girls were going crazy, my girls were all fallen over on the ground, exhausted, devastated. I remember someone had their face in their hands. A lot of them, actually. It was awful. Seconds away from being state champs. Seconds.

Just awful.

Well, anyway, the game wasn't over. Regular season, it would've ended as a draw, but in the playoffs you can't have draws. You need a winner. So there's extra time. I didn't actually know the rules, believe it or not, it being my first year coaching and all, but the ref came over and explained it to me and Carlos. To me, really.

Carlos knew the rules. He'd been coaching forever.

Lisa Roney, East Sycamore: Extra time rules are mostly the same between FIFA and high school. FIFA gives you two 15-minute periods, high school gives you two 10-minute periods. That's the only real difference. If you're still tied up after that, you go to a best of five shootout, same as FIFA.

I didn't actually know any of this at the time. Three years playing high school soccer, and I'd never had a game go to extra time. Which isn't *too* surprising, really. They only happen during the playoffs. Regular season, you just end in a draw. But you can't have a draw in the playoffs, can you? Gotta have a winner.

Anyway, Coach explained it all to us. Gathered the whole team together and told us how it would all work. It's funny, I remember how he had to kind of yell at the team to shut up and pay attention, which was rare for him. We were all still geeked up about Estefania's goal. It had happened like, literally two or three minutes before, so we were just buzzing with the excitement of it. Giggling, happy, talking with each other about it. Chamique and I couldn't stop grinning at each other. The whole team was just buzzing. Now Coach is telling us to cool out and listen? Telling us we've got to play another 20 minutes? It was a little... I guess the word is anti-climactic. We'd just had this huge, huge moment, only to find out, *Well, no, that's not the end of it. Sorry. Gotta play some more.* It was a little weird.

Clementine Thiamale, West Sycamore: It was hard

going out there and playing again. I think everyone would agree. We were just kind of... exhausted, I guess. Emotionally exhausted. Those last 20 minutes – constantly under attack – that would always be difficult. But to go through all that, then give up the tying goal? I felt like a balloon that had been popped. It was terrible. And I think the whole team felt the same. We were all out there, sitting on the field, looking at each other like we couldn't believe it. It was terrible. We were just destroyed.

And then, five minutes later, we're on the field again, playing.

If you can call it playing. Not much happened during those 20 minutes. East was just as tired as us, so, you know, those two extra periods were uneventful. They'd hold the ball for awhile and not do much. We'd hold the ball for awhile and not do much. After ten minutes, we switched sides. It was pretty boring, I guess. My parents said so afterward. They said both teams looked like they just wanted to get through extra time without giving up a goal. Get to the shootout and settle it there. That's how it looked to them. And that's how it felt on the field, too. A couple exhausted teams just trying to make it to the shootout.

And then the extra time was up, the referee was blowing his whistle, and it was time to start the shootout.

C.I. DeMann

The Shootout

Carlos Orostieta, East Sycamore: If you can believe it, I'd only been through one shootout before. It's true! Forty years coaching and only two shootouts! I'd been to the playoffs many times, of course. I'd gone to extra time more than once. But a shootout? Only once before. A first round game, I think it was. We'd won.

But this shootout? Oh, it was much different, much different. For one, it wasn't some first round game, now was it? It was the championship. And secondly, well, you know what happened, eh? Who could have seen that coming? Madness. *[laughs]* Madness!

Susan Douglas, West Sycamore: High school shootout rules are pretty much the same as FIFA rules. Best of five. Put your best five girls out there, let them shoot from the spot. First one team, then the other, back and forth, back and forth. Coach Nolan, she didn't know any of that. *[laughs]* Did she tell you that? She had no idea. She was over there talking to the ref, learning how shootouts worked, then comes over and explains it all to us. *[laughs]* For some reason, I find that really funny, the way she was just kind of figuring it all out on the fly.

So anyway, she had to pick five of us to kick, and decided on me, Martha Sullivan, Destinee Jones, Daniela DeLeon, and, I think one of our center backs, Tamika McKinney. Yeah, that was the five. I don't think it was in that order, though. I can't remember what order she told us to go in.

Nykesha Nolan, West Sycamore: I didn't know what order to put them in. *[laughs]* No idea. That should probably be embarrassing, but whatever, it was my first time. I've read about it since then – the strategies of penalty shootouts – but at the time, I just picked five girls and let them decide the order. Destinee Jones ended up taking charge out on the field. She told everyone when they were going to shoot. Who knows what her logic was. Maybe she just wanted to go first.

Clementine Thiamale, West Sycamore: Destinee kind of ran things. We were all out there at midfield, standing shoulder to shoulder along the midfield line, all of us facing toward the goal. East's girls, they're out there, too. Down the line just a bit, maybe 10 yards down the line, shoulder to shoulder, same as us. We're all out there, the whole team. Well, not the whole team.

Just the eleven of us who were playing. Or the ten field players, I guess. The two keepers, they're down by the goal. You've seen shootouts, you know what they look like.

I'd say we were pretty good mentally. I was, at least. Exhausted, yes, but, you know, not really scared or anything. I didn't feel like I was going to be sick to my stomach or anything. Some of the other girls did. *Felt* like they were going to throw up, that is. No one *actually* threw up. A few were close. And some girls couldn't even watch. It was different for everyone.

Susan Douglas, West Sycamore: Our keeper, Michelle Washington, she was pretty calm, to be honest. I saw Coach talking to her beforehand, pulling her aside for a little pep talk. But Coach was kind of the hyper one and Michelle was the calm one. *[laughs]* Eventually, Coach just shut up and let her go do her thing.

I wouldn't call Michelle the world's best keeper or anything, but for most of the season, she didn't need to be. But then Maria got hurt, and the defense had to get a lot better in a hurry You'd have to give Michelle some credit for that. She raised her game.

And she was great during that shootout, too. Calm, steady. The pressure was unbelievable, and she handled it really, really well.

Chamique Lennox, East Sycamore: It was my first shootout, obviously. Pretty much everything I did that year was my first time doing it. I'm not sure about Michelle.

She was a nice girl. We didn't really talk much, but still, we had little interactions. Before it all started, we were back there on the end line, over to the side. We told each other good luck. That's pretty much all we said to each other. We'd slap hands between shooters. Like, after I faced a shot, I'd be walking back to the end line, she'd be walking into goal, and we'd slap hands or bump fists as we passed. I have no idea if that's how most keepers do it. I imagine when you get to the highest levels, keepers are a little more cutthroat. A little less friendly. I don't know. But Michelle and I were fine. Giving each other little fist bumps seemed the natural thing to do. We were in the same boat. A couple girls both going through this really intense thing. Why be enemies? That's my attitude, at least.

I don't think Hayley would have approved.

Destinee Jones, West Sycamore: Coach let me decide the order. I didn't really have a strategy other than, *Who looks like they're ready to go?* That was pretty much all that went into it. *Who looks ready?*

So we were up first, and I decided to take the first shot. I felt confident. Felt I could go up there, bang it home, and show the other girls how it was done.

My shot was good. I think I put it to the right. Or maybe left. It doesn't matter. East's keeper dove the other way. 1-0, us. I think I probably pumped my fist in the air or something. To be completely honest, I was pretty damn tired. We all were. We'd just played, what, 100 minutes? The full 80, plus the two 10-minute overtimes? And then there was stoppage time, so really it was more like 105, 110 minutes. We were all pretty exhausted. And it was cold as hell, too. Just a bunch of cold, tired girls out there at midfield, watching shot after shot after shot.

After my shot, walking back to midfield, I passed East's shooter, whoever it was taking their first shot. We didn't say anything. I barely looked at her, really. I was thinking about who should go next. Looking at the four girls Coach had chosen, trying to decide who looked the most ready.

They're actually sort of funny, shootouts. The way people look during them. Everyone's a little different. There's 10 girls, of course, all lined up shoulder to shoulder at midfield. Five of them have been picked to shoot, so those five are probably the most into it. Some look eager, some look scared, some... don't really look any way, I guess. Of our five shooters, Martha Sullivan looked the most nervous. She looked pretty miserable, actually. Like she was trying not to puke. Tamika, Susan, Daniela, they all looked fine.

Anyway, that's the shooters. The other five girls, they're just watching. They're just cheering everyone on. But again, there's variety. A lot of them have their elbows linked, all pumped up, super into watching, cheering everyone on. Some are quiet. Nervous. Some are out and out miserable. I told you Martha

Sullivan looked miserable. The other one was Yoreli Ospina. She spent the entire time on her knees. Praying, I guess. She was down on her knees, eyes closed, her hands sort of out in front of her, palms up. I'm not sure if she ever opened her eyes to watch. I remember somebody was next to her, with her hand on Yoreli's shoulder. I think it was Clem. Maybe they were praying together. I don't know.

Anyway, walking back from my spot kick, I thought Daniela looked the most ready to go, so I picked her to shoot second.

Kaitlyn Baker, East Sycamore: West shot first. Their captain, Destinee Jones. Her shot was good. 1-0. Then came Ye-Jee Park, our right winger. Good. 1-1. Next was their girl, I don't remember who, but she hit hers. 2-1, West. Then I was up.

I've taken a few PKs over the years – you know, for penalties and such – but shootouts, they're a totally different thing. Totally different feel. For starters, during a normal PK, everyone's all gathered around the box, waiting for you to shoot, but during a shootout, everyone's way back at midfield. You're totally alone. You've got that long walk to the spot, and then it's just you and the goalie. You've sort of got the referee there, of course. And your team's keeper is over there on the end line, off to the side, waiting for her turn. But mostly, it feels like you and the opposing goalie are the only two people in the world. You make that long walk to the spot, you get the ball set, the ref blows the whistle, and you take your shot. Just you and the goalie and the ball. It's kind of cool, really.

So anyway, my shot. I don't know if there's a perfect strategy to it. I figure, just kick it hard and don't miss. *[laughs]* That sounds a little stupid, I guess, but it's true. Some people try and finesse it a little too much, and it bites them in the ass. They'll kick it a little too soft, and the goalie will knock it away. Or maybe they'll try to get it so close to the post that they end up sending it wide. So my attitude is, don't get cute. Kick it hard, kick it on target, make the keeper work. So that's what I did. Kicked it to the right, I think. Goalie went the other way. 2-2.

The crowd was going crazy, by the way. I told you how we were in their football stadium, right? Big crowd. Big. Probably 50/50, us and them. We had a lot of fans travel, since it was just across town. So, you know, the whole stadium was just going crazy during the whole shootout. It was pretty fun. It would get super-quiet right before the kick, then half the crowd would explode right after, depending if it was a hit or a miss. We were the same way out at midfield. Right before a shot, we'd all be leaning forward, up on our toes. Then, after, we'd be cheering or not, depending on how it went. It was fun. And also kind of exhausting, I guess. That kind of tension, over and over and over, it takes a lot out of you. And it's not like we weren't tired already, having played a full game and then extra time. I'll tell you what, by the time it was all done? I was as tired as you can possibly imagine. Just went home and collapsed. Utterly exhausted.

11v11

Okay, where was I? I made my kick, it was 2-2. The West girl goes up there and hits her shot. 3-2, them. Next for us is Mary Ogwumike. Just *barely* made hers. West's goalkeeper actually got a hand on that one, but not enough to keep it out. Still tied, 3-3.

Martha Sullivan, West Sycamore: God, Michelle was *so close*. Dove the right way, got a hand to the shot, but not quite enough. The ball was deflected a tiny bit, but not much. Not much at all. You could see how frustrated Michelle was. She was diving over and over and over. I don't know how many times she hit the ground. She must have been bruised and sore after it was all over. And then when she finally gets her hand on a shot, it's not enough. Super frustrating. Not just for her, but for all of us.

So it was 3-3. Susan Douglas was our next shooter. Destinee was picking the order. Did you know that? Yeah, Coach kind of stayed out of it. Destinee made all the decisions out there on the field.

So, Susan was next. I remember watching her walk to the spot, I was thinking, *Kick it hard, Susan. Kick it hard.* Hell, I may have yelled it out loud, I can't remember. I just know that Susan had a tendency to play a little soft. You know, soft passes, soft shots. That's not always a problem. Sometimes a soft little pass is exactly what you need. But shooting penalties? I was really worried she'd be too soft. Worried the keeper would just knock it away.

In the end, Susan went right down the middle. Goalie

dove left or right, I can't remember, but Susan put it right down the middle, nice and soft. I guess soft works sometimes, right?

So, that made it 4-3 us. Very, very tense. God, I was so friggin' nervous. You have no idea. I honestly wanted to vomit. It was awful. I had my arms linked with the girls on either side of me, and I was just so, so nervous, the whole time.

Anyway, it's 4-3 us. East's girl is walking out to the spot. Big girl. Their forward, I think. The crowd's cheering like crazy. The team's cheering, too. "You got this, Michelle! You got this!" That sort of thing. I'm silent, trying not to puke.

So, their girl walks to the spot, Michelle's in goal, everyone gets quiet... and the girl misses! Sends it super-high, way over the cross bar.

Okay, all this next stuff, I remember it like it was yesterday. Like it was *yesterday*.

After their girl misses, there's like two different worlds. There's the *real* world and then there's *my* world. In the real world, the crowd's going absolutely bananas. Around me, the entire team's going bananas. It's madness. Because, you know, there's just one more shooter. Our fifth shooter. And if she hits it, we win. We're state champs. State friggin' champs.

The problem? *I'm* the fifth shooter. And I feel like I'm going to collapse, right there on the field. Around me, everyone's going nuts, but in my world, it's super-silent. Super-still. All I can hear is my pulse in my ear. God, it was awful. *Awful.* Destinee's there, pointing at me, all smiles, hand on my shoulder, telling me to go take my shot, go win the championship for us. I assume that's what she was saying, at least. I couldn't hear a damn thing. Honestly, I'm not exaggerating any of this. How I didn't vomit, I have no idea. I'm really not cut out for big moments like that. Not cut out for it at all.

So, yeah... there I was, walking up to the spot. The ball's sitting there. Really, it was the state title sitting there. All I had to do was hit the shot, and we'd be champs.

And I hit the post.

God, it was so awful. I've relived it over and over. I've thought about that stupid ball sitting there. I've thought about my run up to the ball. I've thought about my foot hitting the ball. I've thought about the keeper diving the wrong way. I've thought about how I could instantly tell, *Oh, crap, this is gonna be close. Oh, crap, no, no, no, don't hit the post, no, no, no.* It all happened in less than a second, but I remember it all. I couldn't convince the ball to shift just a little. It hit the post. Hit it dead solid perfect. Bounced off to the side. All the East fans go crazy, all the West fans go silent. I fall to my knees right there at the penalty spot, just crushed. Just destroyed.

The championship was right there for me to take. If I hit that ball an inch differently, maybe half an inch, we're champs, and I'm the hero. Instead, I'm on my knees, my face in my hands, wondering how this could've happened to me.

Eventually, I stood up and walked back to midfield. The girls took me in, linked elbows with me again, but jeez, I could barely look at them. I really... that was one of the worst moments of my life. I mean it. It's stuck with me to this day. Half an inch. That's how close I was to winning State. Half an inch.

Nykesha Nolan, West Sycamore: To be honest, if there was one girl on that team who you'd have called a sure thing, it was Martha Sullivan. I was *sure* she'd nail it. Sure we were gonna be State champs.

But nope. She hits the post. I couldn't believe it. *She* couldn't believe it. Just sank to her knees right there on the spot.

So, that made the shootout 4-3. Martha walked back to the center of the pitch, and the next East girl walked to the spot. The fifth and final East girl.

There's still hope, of course. We're not completely dead. If Michelle Washington can get her first save, we win, right? We win 4-3. But no, she dives the wrong way and it's 4-4.

Well, at this point it gets a little funny, because, of course, I was still a first year coach, and I still didn't know how things worked. *[laughs]* Just like I hadn't known how a penalty shootout worked, now I didn't know what happened if you went through your five shooters and were tied. I mean, it's a best of five shootout, right? And we'd finished in a tie, 4-4. What now? Do we have them shoot again? Another best of five? I had no idea. *[laughs]*

So, the ref's out there, pointing at the spot, telling the next shooter to step up. The girls at midfield are looking at each other like, *Wait, we have to shoot, too?* They didn't know what to do. *[laughs]* Fortunately, Destinee Jones took over. She just pointed at our left back Constanza Valenzuela and said, "You're up." Ref's pointing at the spot, telling them to hurry up, and Connie's slowly walking toward goal, wondering how she'd ended up there. It was a really weird situation, none of us knowing quite what was happening. It really felt like we were making it up as we went along.

Catalina Forero, East Sycamore: Yeah, we had no idea. The original five, they knew they were gonna kick, but the rest of us? We thought our job was just to stand out there at midfield and cheer. You know, maybe link elbows or something. That was our job. Cheering. And then, all of a sudden, the ref's telling us we've got to shoot, too? Kind of an eye-opener, you know?

Estefania Higuain, she hadn't even been watching. Did you know that? She spent the entire shootout facing the other way, a towel over her head. I swear! Didn't see a single shot. She was a few girls down the line from me, eyes closed, towel over her head, facing the opposite goal. Now Kaitlyn Baker's like, "Hey, Estefania, look

alive, we may need you to shoot, okay?" *[laughs]*
Estefania gave a little nod. You could see the towel on
her head bob up and down real quick, but that was it.
[laughs] It really is kind of funny. Not that funny at
the time, I guess, but looking back on it, yeah. Kind of
funny.

So anyway, the ref's telling us we're gonna have to
shoot. Coach is yelling out to us what order he wants
us to go in, and I'm up first. So, um... I guess... who hit
our last shot? Vilma Aguilar. She made it 4-4. West
sends out their next girl – who I guess at this point is
their *sixth* shooter, right? So their girl goes up there
and hits her shot. 5-4, them. And I'm up.

Well, I'm nervous, of course. How could I not be? As
I'm walking from midfield to the spot, the fans are
going nuts. It's cold, we're tired, I'm nervous. Walking
up to the spot, I'm not entirely sure about the rules, so I
ask the ref – he's standing there by the spot, waiting for
me – I ask him, "So, do we go through another five
girls?" And he's like, "Only if we need to." So I'm
like, "You mean it could end before that?" He says, "It
could end right now, if you miss your shot." And I'm
like, *Jeez, put a little pressure on a girl, why don't you?*
I didn't say that, but I thought it.

Shootouts are brutal, you know? Those first few girls,
they don't have total pressure on them. If one of them
misses, it's not the end of the game. But when you get
past them? Into girl six, seven, eight? Every one of
them is do or die. Especially if you're going second,
like we were.

Well, anyway, the ball's there, the fans are going crazy, I'm standing there, looking at the ball, looking at their goalie, wondering if I should do something to psych her out, if there's some secret way to do penalties that I don't know about, but in the end, I just run up and kick it as hard as I can. I kick it left, their goalie dives the other way, and it's good. 5-5. On to the next two girls.

Lisa Roney, East Sycamore: When Catalina came back to midfield, she told us all what the ref had told her, that the shootout would go pair by pair until someone got the advantage. I'd been hoping it would end before my turn came up, but since Coach Orostieta had already picked our order, and I was in the next pair, I knew I'd have to go. Honestly, when you're not one of the first five girls, you just assume you won't have to kick. But here I was... what was I, seventh? Yeah, Catalina was sixth, I was seventh. The seventh girl, and I was gonna have to kick. Crazy.

So West's girl goes out before me, of course. You know, I think it's worth mentioning that, as much as I'm complaining that I had to kick, Chamique was part of *every single kick.* She had to step in there for each of the first five girls, then the sixth, then the seventh, every single time. So, you know, don't feel too bad for me, having to do this really stressful thing one time. Chamique was dealing with the stress over and over and over. West's goalkeeper, too. As bad as shootouts are for us, they're a thousand times worse for the keepers. Step in there, get all stressed out, dive one way or the other, hit the ground, pick yourself up, then do it again and again and again. God bless keepers, right? They're the real heroes.

Carlos Orostieta, East Sycamore: Shootouts are a funny thing for keepers. Yes, they're stressful. Yes, they're tiring. Yes, you hit the ground over and over and over. All of that is difficult, without a doubt. But there's another side to it. In a lot of ways, the keeper can only be the hero. They can't be the goat.

Think about it, my friend. In a PK situation, how often does the keeper make the save? About 10-20% of the time. That's the average. So, one out of five shots. Really, more like one out of 10. At least 80, 90% of the time, the ball's going into the net. Everyone knows it. So if a goalkeeper faces a five-person shootout and doesn't make a single save, nobody's going to really hold that against her, you see? No one's going to say, "Oh, she's a bum!"

But if she makes one save? She's a hero. Two saves? She's super-human! *[laughs]*

That's what I told Chamique before the shootout. That's what Hayley Swanson told her. We told her it would be stressful, it would be exhausting, and she'd be sore from hitting the ground so much, but if she could, she should try to relax. Because no matter how it went, she wouldn't be the goat. She could only be the hero.

Lisa Roney, East Sycamore: So anyway, West's girl goes out there and hits her shot. Chamique, she guesses wrong again. Dives the wrong way, hits the ground,

picks herself up. Man, was she sore and tired after.
Crazy.

And that made it, what? 6-5? And I'm up. Catalina –
we'd had our elbows locked – she gives me a little pat
on the back, and I head up to the spot. Long walk.
Very tense. Just like with Catalina, if I miss it, we lose.
Game over. State title's theirs.

I don't really remember what I was thinking, there at the
spot.   I probably didn't think much of anything.
Knowing me, I just backed up, came forward, and
whacked it.   You know, big dumb center back.
[laughs] No thought at all, probably. But, thank
heavens, it was good. 6-6. We're still alive. On to the
next pair of girls.

Estefania Higuain, East Sycamore: I was after Lisa.
I was hoping it would be decided by then, but it wasn't.
Still tied. And I guess we were the seventh or eighth
pair of girls. So when Lisa hit her shot, I knew I'd have
to shoot.

I didn't see anything, of course. I was still facing away.
Still had the towel over my head, still had my eyes
closed. Sloane Bird was next to me. She was our
defensive midfielder. Nice girl. She was there next to
me in line, her arm linked in mine, only she was facing
forward. She was telling me what was going on.
Giving me play-by-play, I guess you could say. Not
everything, but just enough. "Kaitlyn's next. She's
walking up. She hit it. Their girl's going up now. She
hit it." Sort of like that.

When we got past the original five girls, and we suddenly realized we might have to shoot, too, that definitely made things more nervous, but I didn't change anything. I was still facing the other way, still not looking, still with the towel over my head. People have asked me if I regret that, if I wish I could've seen it, but no, I don't regret it. I was too nervous. I could barely handle the tension facing away. If I'd been watching, I probably would have passed out.

To be honest, I spent a lot of that time thinking about Hugo. Wondering if he was watching. If watching games was something dead people could do. He would have loved it, of course. So much drama. Me scoring that late goal? Extra time? A shootout? A shootout that goes past the original five girls? He would have loved it. I couldn't watch, but he sure would have. He would have loved the whole thing.

So that's what I thought about. Hugo and what he'd think of it all.

When Sloane told me Lisa had hit her shot, I knew I'd have to shoot. That was tough. My stomach was really twisted up then.

Sloane told me the West girl was walking to the spot, then the stadium got quiet, just like it did every time. But after the shot it got *super*-loud, much more than usual, and Sloane was jumping around like crazy, shaking me. "She saved it! Chamique saved it!"

11v11

I still had the towel over my head, was still facing the other end, but, yeah, I could tell that this cheer was much louder. The whole stadium was going nuts. My teammates were going nuts. Chamique had finally made a save, and all we had to do was hit our next shot, and we were champions.

And it was my turn.

Well, there was nothing to do about it, was there? It was my turn. I had to go. Kaitlyn was telling me to go shoot. "Go win it for us," she said. Sloane was squeezing my arm. "Go win it, Estefania," she said.

I can't tell you how tough that walk was, how much my stomach was twisting. I took the towel off my head, handed it to Sloane, and started walking to the spot. I was almost trembling, I was so nervous. Some people, they probably love moments like that, but me, I was not happy at all. It was all too much. I didn't want it. Not at all.

But I walked to the spot. I made sure the ball was set on the spot. I thought, *Okay, it's just like at practice. Just kick it like it's practice.* I took a few steps back, then ran up and kicked it.

I kicked it toward the left post. It was hard enough, but not far enough over. Not far enough toward the post. Their keeper, she guessed right. She dove the right way, and I immediately realized, *Oh no, she's going to get it.* She did, too. Got it easily. It practically hit her in the chest. Not nearly far enough toward the post.

Not nearly. She dove, got it, and pushed it straight back toward me.

The crowd, they went wild. The keeper, she jumped up and screamed. I didn't really do much. I was crushed, of course, but, what was I going to do? Fall over and start crying? No, I just turned and started walking back to midfield. Back to my team.

They were disappointed, of course. The West girls were jumping up and down, happy they were still alive. My girls, they just looked tired. None of them said anything mean. Sloane was like, "It's okay. We'll get them." I took the towel from her and put it back over my head. Faced the opposite goal like before. Closed my eyes.

It was a bad moment, sure, but it didn't destroy me. It wasn't the worst thing to happen to me that year, you know? When you compare it to a dying brother, missing a penalty shot doesn't seem quite so bad.

Clementine Thiamale, West Sycamore: Watching their girl walk up there and take her shot, oh my goodness, the tension! It was terrible. Just awful. I had my hand on Yoreli's shoulder – she was still down on her knees, praying – and, I swear, I probably gave her shoulder bruises, I was squeezing it so hard. I never asked her what sort of prayers she was saying. I kind of imagine it was Hail Marys or Our Fathers or something, but I'm not sure. Maybe it was more specific than that. Maybe she was praying, *Oh, Lord, our girl just missed. Make their girl miss, too.* I don't know, that seems a little harsh. It was probably just Hail Marys.

Anyway, whatever she prayed, it must have gotten through, because Michelle saved it. Matched East's save with a save of her own. Wow. So exciting! Honestly, that was such a moment.

Unfortunately – or maybe fortunately – I was up next. Gosh, what number was I? Eighth? Ninth? Tenth? I really don't know. I didn't think there was any chance they'd get to me. Shootouts just don't go that long, do they? Heck, sometimes they don't even make it through the original five girls. But ours just kept going and going and going. What a game!

Okay, so, it was my turn. I remember looking into the stands while I walked to the spot. Saw Mama and Papa and Curtis. He waved at me. My parents didn't. They looked too nervous. Very serious faces. I think I waved at them, trying to pretend I wasn't nervous.

My kick was nothing special. I went right. Their keeper didn't even dive. Did she think I was going down the middle? I think she was probably just tired. She'd been diving over and over and over. Maybe she was just sick of hitting the ground.

So the crowd cheered. Walking back to midfield, I waved at my parents again, and this time they waved back. They told me I had a huge smile on my face, which I can believe. I was so relieved. So glad to be done with it.

When I got back to our line, I grabbed my same spot, next to Yoreli. She gave me a high five and a congratulations, then closed her eyes, and started praying again.

Carlos Orostieta, East Sycamore: Let me tell you, my friend, by this point, I wasn't sure the shootout would *ever* end. *[laughs]* That sounds like a joke, but I tell you, I really wasn't sure. They hit, we hit. They miss, we miss. Their keeper finally gets a save, our keeper finally gets a save. *[laughs]* I wish you could have been there. Absolutely incredible. What a game!

So where were we? The ninth pairing? That was Bird, I believe. Yes. Sloane Bird. I don't recall her shot perfectly, but I know it was good. So it's on to the tenth pair of girls! *[laughs]* Incredible. Just incredible. Do you know the record for longest shootout? I don't, but I tell you, ours must have been close.

Okay, tenth round. Who shot for them? Oh, yes, it was the one who was praying. I remember her well. She spent the whole shootout on her knees, praying. Probably never thought she'd have to shoot, but there she was, climbing to her feet and walking to the spot. She did well, too. Marched to the spot and sank her shot. Very professional.

Next, I believe, was our right back, Sylvia Danielson. And do you know, she was very calm, too. Very professional. Spot kicks are a funny thing, aren't they? Sometimes the players you'd think are a sure thing, they get nervous, they can't take the pressure. Then the players you choose last, the ones you don't even think will take their kick, they are the ones who look the best.

Soccer is a funny little game sometimes. A funny little game.

Nykesha Nolan, head coach, West Sycamore: After awhile, there's only so stressed out you can be, I guess. You can only hold your breath so many times. You can only tense your body so many times. This was the tenth round? We were exhausted. All of us. So when the East girl walked up there and sank it, nobody freaked. We slumped a little. They cheered a little, but it was maybe a little less than before. There's only so much drama you can take.

So, at this point, it's a little funny. It's our turn again, but we'd gone through all our players. Destinee is out there at midfield, and she yells over to me, "There's no one left! We've all shot!" I look over at Carlos, like *What do we do now?* He kind of shrugs at me, so we both look to the ref, call him over. He doesn't even come halfway, he just yells at us, "Keepers gotta shoot!" Carlos and I, we're looking at each other like, *You've gotta be kidding me. Our goalkeepers have got to shoot?* And we both started laughing. I swear. We were both exhausted, the tension was so high, and we just started laughing, rolling our eyes. It was almost nice, that little moment we had there. Two coaches confused and tired and at their wit's end. He was really nice at the end, when we shook hands. It was a hell of a game, one for the history books, and we both knew it.

So anyway, keepers gotta shoot. So I'm yelling that to Michelle Washington, and she's looking at me all confused. I yell it again, and she really doesn't understand, she's just shaking her head. Then Destinee Jones starts yelling at her from midfield, telling her she's got to shoot a PK, and she finally realizes what's going on. *[laughs]* Her eyes went so wide, it was almost funny. I remember laughing a tiny bit, the poor thing. But anyway, eyes wide, she pulls her gloves off. Wait, did she pull her gloves off? She may have just shot with her gloves on. Probably did. Anyway, she walks to the spot, puts the ball down, and takes her shot.

Chamique Lennox, East Sycamore: I'll never forget that moment when we realized we had to shoot. I was in goal, waiting for their next shooter, getting myself psyched up. It was cold as hell. Michelle was on the end line, waiting her turn. There was some confusion going on. People trying to figure out who was next. I just stood there in goal, waiting, trying to block it out, really. Just trying to keep my game face, I guess.

And then the West coach was yelling at Michelle, telling her she had to shoot. I was like, *No. That can't be right. Goalies don't shoot PKs. Somebody's got this wrong.*

But they just kept telling her that. Her coach, her captain, the ref. They were all saying it. "Keepers gotta shoot." Michelle and I were looking at each other, eyes wide. Honestly, it was almost funny. If the situation hadn't been so tense, we probably would've laughed. We didn't, though. She just started walking out to the spot, looking like she didn't quite believe it.

It was weird, setting up for that shot. I mean, I'd faced player after player after player, so, you know, I was used to what it looked like. Same uniform, same basic look. Now, suddenly, there's a girl out there wearing a goalie uniform. And gloves. It just looked wrong. Totally wrong.

It actually kind of messed with my head a little. I'd sort of gotten my game face on, gotten my mind ready to face a shot, and now I'm looking at a goalie. It threw me off. I remember, I actually took a moment. I stepped out of goal and did a little circle on the end line. I was just kind of, I don't know, giving myself a pep talk or something. You know, something like, *You got this, Chamique. It's no different. Just another PK. You got this.*

Then I walked back into goal and faced her.

Maria Solana, West Sycamore: Oh, the tension! I could barely take it. Coach Nolan, she was next to me, and she'd been standing most of the time, but when Michelle walked up to take her kick, I remember Coach crouching down next to me, her hands over her mouth. She said something to me, very low, something like, "Oh, Maria. This is too much. Just too much." Something like that. I think we all felt that way, all of us on the sideline. The emotions, they were too much.

Michelle's kick, it was... well, I am sorry to say, she

didn't do too well with it. It wasn't much of a shot. She hit the grass a little. Scuffed it. East's goalie, she saved it. She didn't get a good jump on it, but she didn't need to, the shot was so weak. She saved it no problem.

I remember Coach putting her face in her hands then. I was there with my leg on my scooter, and Coach was crouched down, face in her hands. I felt so bad for her. I think I may have given her a pat on the back.

I wish I could have given Michelle a pat on the back, too. She was out at the spot, crouched down like Coach. To tell the truth, we were all sagging a bit. The whole team. The girls on the field, the girls on the sideline with me. It was a bad moment.

But the game wasn't over, of course. Michelle had missed, but East's goalkeeper still had to shoot. And I remember thinking, *Maybe she will shoot it as poorly as Michelle did.* So all of us on the sideline, we all started cheering again. Clapping for Michelle. Telling her she could make the save, she could keep us alive. Keep the shootout going.

Catalina Forero, East Sycamore: Watching Chamique walk to the spot, I was thinking, *Man, she shouldn't even be here. It should be Hayley Swanson up there.* Biggest moment of the year, and it's some little freshman kid who hadn't even wanted to go out for the team! Did you know that? She wasn't gonna go out for the team, but Coach talked her into it. Told her she'd probably never even play.

Crazy, right? She goes from "You'll never even play," straight to "You're gonna have to take a penalty kick in the state championship game."

What a story.

Martha Sullivan, West Sycamore: You want to know something? By that point, I was actually feeling sort of halfway calm. I mean, for most of that shootout, I was trying not to puke, but...

You know what I think it was? I think it was my miss. When I missed my kick, I think at that point, I was like, *Welp, you screwed up, Martha. You blew it. Nothing to do now but watch.* And it wasn't a good kind of indifference. I wasn't cool and calm and okay with everything. It was more like, *You probably lost State for your team. Nothing you can do about it now.* That's pretty awful, I know, but it's how I felt.

So when Michelle missed her shot, I didn't freak. I didn't lose hope. My hope was already lost. And how could I blame Michelle? I was already blaming myself.

So, you know, when East's keeper was standing there, lining up her shot, other people were probably freaking out then, but I wasn't. I was just kind of standing there hating myself, blaming myself for the whole damn thing.

Chamique Lennox, East Sycamore: I was nervous, sure. Wanting to puke? No, not really. I mean, I'd just gotten done facing, what was it, 10 penalty shots?

After all that stress, taking the actual shot wasn't really that bad.

I heard my dad yelling at me from the stands. He had this way of yelling, he'd put a bunch of bass in his voice so it would really, really carry. He'd cup his hands around his mouth, too. So when I heard that deep voice yelling, "You got this, Chamique! You got this!" I knew it was him.

That helped.

So, erm... what to say about the actual shot? The ball was there at the spot. The ref was over to my left, watching. Michelle was in goal, waiting. That was weird. It was weird watching her shoot, it was weird watching her wait for *me* to shoot. Just weirdness all around.

But, um, anyway... the shot. I backed up a few steps, took a quick look at goal, and decided to kick it left. Why left? I don't know. Why not?

So I ran forward, kicked it as hard as I could, and... it was good. We won. We were state champions.

Destinee Jones, West Sycamore: I kind of collapsed. Just fell to my knees right there at midfield. You know, face in my hands, trying not to cry, the whole thing. I heard the crowd cheering, the East players celebrating, but I didn't see any of it.

I don't know how long I was like that. Too long. I

remember I had to talk myself back to reality. I was like, *Pull it together, Destinee. You're the captain. Don't be a martyr. Don't let this break you. Your team needs you.*

In truth, that's what got me to my feet, the thought that my team needed me. So I stood up, wiped my face, and got myself together. My team needed me.

Kaitlyn Baker, East Sycamore: I kind of lost my mind, to be honest. When Chamique put that shot home, we just raced forward, the whole team, me leading the charge. God, did we mob her. Did we knock her over? I don't think so. I think she kept her feet. But oh, Lord, did she get mobbed. Hugged by everyone, all at the same time. The bench players, too. Was Coach there? Probably not. He was too old for that sort of thing. We weren't, though. We were just laughing and dancing and cheering. Just this huge screaming pile of girls. So much fun.

It was interesting, because first there was the one big celebration, and then it kind of broke into a bunch of smaller celebrations. First I'd be hugging and laughing with these two girls, then I'd be with a couple other girls. It was like that for everyone. Just this huge party, constantly shifting and changing. Such a great moment. I loved it.

Maria Solana, West Sycamore: It was terrible. I was there on the sideline, and everyone was sort of wandering around looking miserable, and I just felt so... useless. Because these were my teammates, you know, and I really cared about them. I wanted to help, but what could I do? Half the girls, with my English, I couldn't even talk to them. I had all these kind words, and I couldn't even use them. Also, I was rolling around on this stupid little scooter thing, so that was very slow and awkward and frustrating. And I hadn't even *played*, so who was I to say anything? I was no one. It was terrible.

Mostly, I remember thinking that I couldn't wait for the next season to start, so we could try again. Isn't that funny? A few months earlier, I hadn't even known there was this thing called "State." But now, it was the most important thing in the world. I remember very clearly rolling around on my scooter, everyone miserable, and thinking, *Next year, we'll win it. Next year I will play and we will win it all.*

Estefania Higuain, East Sycamore: It was so fun, the dancing and laughing and hugging. It was all sort of a blur, to be honest. A little like when I scored the goal at the end of regulation. Both times, my brain turned off, and there was just happiness. Fun.

I think that lasted maybe five minutes, maybe more, but it finally broke up a tiny bit and then I realized that all these other people were on the field with us. People from the stands. Parents, friends, people like that. I was looking around for my family and finally saw them over by the sideline, all bunched together. Everyone was there. My parents, my uncles, my cousins, everyone.

I went over to them, and they all cheered and gave me hugs. I think it was when I hugged my mother that I started crying. It was. She said something like, "Hugo would be so proud of you, my love. I know he's watching," and I just fell to pieces. It was like popping a balloon or something. I'd been holding it all in, I guess, but that was when I finally burst.

We left right after that. I'm not sure what happened with the rest of the team. Celebrated all night, probably. But I went home to be with my family.

I hope it's true that dead people can watch what we do here on Earth. Hugo would have loved that shootout. If only there had been a fight between Kaitlyn and Catalina, right? *[laughs]* Then it would have been perfect!

Clementine Thiamale, West Sycamore: My parents came down onto the field. Not to the center of the pitch, but over on the sideline. Curtis was with them. They were sad, of course. So was I.

My papa tried to pick up my spirits. He told me how proud he was of me, how well I'd played, how close we had been. I think he said something about how, when he'd played, he'd never been that close to winning a trophy. It was a nice thing to say, but the truth is, it didn't really help so much at the time.

Having Curtis there was nice, though. That helped a little. Having him there with my family, them all getting along so well. I think he even held my hand in front of them. I don't think he was brave enough to kiss me, but a hand hold was nice.

Chamique Lennox, East Sycamore: It was pretty crazy. People were everywhere, all over the field. I got a lot of hugs, a lot of backslaps. It was all kind of a blur.

I do remember Hayley coming up to me at some point. She told me how proud she was of me. Said something like, "This will be your team next year. You'll be ready for it. You're *already* ready for it." Stuff like that.

She was so good to me that year. A lot of people – especially elite players like her – if they'd gotten hurt like she had, they'd have just abandoned me. Just walked away and let me sink or swim. But Hayley didn't. She worked so closely with me, taught me so much in those few weeks.

I know she's really private and is probably not gonna do an interview for this book, but hopefully she'll read it, at least. I'd just like to tell her thanks. We wouldn't have won that championship without her helping me the way she did. It's a fact. She was part of the championship, even if she couldn't play.

Martha Sullivan, West Sycamore: I was trying my hardest just to leave. My parents were there, and I was getting all my stuff together as fast as I could, not really talking to anyone. I just wanted to go home and feel sorry for myself. That's all I wanted. But Destinee got hold of me first. I think we were actually on the way to the parking lot when she found me. She came racing up behind me, calling my name.

I don't remember everything she said. It was basically like, "Listen, I just want you to know how important you were to this team." Something like that. You know, "You were huge to our offense. You scored so many important goals. We wouldn't have made it here without you." Stuff like that.

I didn't want to hear it, not at the time. I just wanted to go home. But I did hear her. Her words did make an impact. At home that night and in the days after, I kept thinking about what she had said. And it helped.

Destinee was a good captain. And a good person. Make sure you print that. She should know.

Catalina Forero, East Sycamore: The celebration went on for a long time. It was cold as hell, of course, but we didn't care. We were gonna celebrate. There was the hugging and the dancing, of course, but there were also the families who wanted to take photos. Solo photos, group photos. My God, how many shots did we take with the whole team together? A thousand? The trophy was there in the center of us, the state championship trophy. Everyone wanted a piece of that. People kissing it, pretending to drink from it, holding it like a baby or something. It was great. I'm not sure who was the ringleader. Lisa and Chamique were both having a lot of fun. Lisa especially. She was fun.

I remember Kaitlyn, she was funny. She was clearly

happy, you know, but... I don't know, she was kind of in a daze, too. Like she couldn't believe it was real. Like, she'd been working so hard and so intensely for so long, and now it had really happened, and she wasn't sure how to deal with it. That's how she looked. Happy, but dazed.

I'll tell you what, if you need to go to war, make sure you've got someone like Kaitlyn Baker on your side. That girl was something else. MVP, I'd say. Not for the game – that would probably be Chamique – but for the season? Kaitlyn would get my vote. *[laughs]* And I started out hating her guts! *[laughs]*

Susan Douglas, West Sycamore: There wasn't much to do but get my stuff and go home. The East girls were all celebrating, of course, but I had no interest in watching any of that. Plus, I was exhausted. And cold. And hungry. How long did the game last? That shootout felt like a complete game all by itself. So I was exhausted. Hungry. Cold. Sad. Ready to leave.

The Galtons came down to the field to find me. That was a first. I'd seen plenty of parents pick up plenty of kids, but never for me. Grandma never did. So that was pretty cool. And surprising. They were amazing. The first people to really treat me like family. The first since Grandma died, at least.

That was a messed up year, you know? Mom dies, Grandma dies, foster home after foster home. Can you imagine me trying to get through all that without the team? I can't. I'd have broken, I know it.

It wasn't perfect. The team wasn't perfect, the season wasn't perfect, far from it. But still, without it? Who knows where I'd be? Who knows how bad things would've gotten?

Worst year of my life, and the team got me through it. They were my family. They were pretty much all I had.

Lisa Roney, East Sycamore: The celebration petered out after awhile. Everyone got their photos and held the cup, said their goodbyes and wandered off with their families. Chamique's cousins were there for awhile. The two little boys I told you about earlier? The giggly boys? Them. They were running around the field, kicking a ball. Just goofing off. Being kids. But, yeah, eventually they took off, and all the families took off, and then there were just a few of us left. I think it was just four of us. Me and Chamique. Catalina and Hayley. Just sitting at midfield, talking. We didn't want to leave. Didn't want the night to end.

I remember it was really freakin' cold, and I was complaining that we should go somewhere warm, but Catalina was like, "Hell with that. I'm never leaving this field. Never. Put some more clothes on." I think I was wearing, like, two jackets, and two or three pairs of sweatpants. I looked like a big marshmallow girl. It was funny.

It's not like we did anything special. Just hung out. Sat at midfield. Talked. Talked about the season. The future. Catalina and Hayley, they were seniors, so, you know, they were talking about how it was all over. How college wouldn't be the same. Me and Chamique, we talked about coming back the next year. Wondering if the team would be good without all the seniors. Without Coach.

It was sort of sad to see that year end. That sounds stupid, right? I mean, we'd just won State. What more could I possibly want, right? *[laughs]* But I don't know... it was never the same after that. The new coach they brought in, he was fine, I guess, but he was no Carlos Orostieta. And without Catalina by my side? It was all really different. Really different. And we could see it coming that night. We knew it was the end of an era.

East hasn't won a state title since then, you know. Maybe they never will. How many did Coach win? Six? Seven? Eight? That game, it was the end of an era. We knew it, the four of us hanging out there at midfield. I think we didn't want to leave the stadium because leaving would have made it official. Nobody put it into those words, exactly, but yeah, that was it. We knew. That night was the end of something special.

Nykesha Nolan, West Sycamore: I stayed awhile. It was cold as can be, but I stayed. I wanted to watch East get their trophy. Wanted to watch them celebrate. It was fuel. Fuel to drive me the next year. To get us back there and win the damn thing. And I was determined to get us back. I watched East lift that trophy so I could imagine my girls lifting it the next year.

That season was something else, wasn't it? I'd never played a game of soccer in my life, and there I was coaching it. And only because it was something to do. *[laughs]* Something to coach in the fall. And then Maria Solana happened. Destinee Jones happened. Martha Sullivan. Susan Douglas. Clementine. We're winning, I'm falling in love with the sport, falling in love with the team. Next thing you know, we're in the state final, almost winning it. It's crazy. The whole story is nuts. But, man, I wouldn't trade it for anything.

So anyway, after the game – hell, the whole rest of that night, driving home, getting ready for bed, whatever – I was thinking about next year. Who was graduating, who'd be coming back, how we'd play, our strengths, our weaknesses. Watching East lift that trophy, it stoked my fire. I was determined. We were gonna get back to that title game. And next time, we were gonna win it.

Carlos Orostieta, East Sycamore: Oh, my friend, let me tell you, driving home that night was so strange. So very strange. I didn't know whether to laugh or cry.

The win, oh, what a win it was! You'll never see another game like that, I can assure you. Thinking of those girls out there, fighting so hard, never giving up, oh, it made me so proud. So proud.

But then I would remember that it was the last time I would be there to coach them. When the team gathered the next year for their first practice, it would be somebody else standing before them. That was a difficult thought, I can tell you.

And it was like that all night. *Oh, I'll have a chance to travel. But do I want to travel? Wouldn't I rather meet all these new players? Yes, but I won't have all the pressure to win. But I'll miss the pressure, won't I? I'll miss fighting it out each week.* Oh, this. Oh, that. Back and forth, all night. My wife, I don't know how she puts up with me. She told me, "This is why you should retire, Carlos. You've been fighting this battle for forty years. It's time to step away. Let someone else fight."

She was right, of course. I see that now. But in the moment? Very hard, very hard.

Well, none of that matters to you, does it? An old man retiring, that is not your story. Your story is the team. And such a team. Such a team! Catalina Forero and Lisa Roney in the middle. Hayley Swanson, one of the all-time greats, behind them. Chamique Lennox. Who would have seen her coming? Estefania Higuain, the poor thing. And, of course, Kaitlyn Baker. Ha! Coming in first day and taking over! Such a story.

Yes, I coached for 40 years. 40 different teams. But that last team? Yes, I would say they were my best. It was a good way to end things, I think. A good way to end.

Epilogue: 10 Years Later

Nykesha Nolan is still coaching three sports. The soccer team won State the following year, has made the playoffs six of 10 years, and is now considered one of the premier girls soccer programs in the state. The softball team has made the playoffs four times and won State once. The basketball team hasn't won State yet, but she thinks this current team has a real shot. She's looking forward to adding one more trophy to the school's trophy case. She wants to fill that thing.

Carlos Orostieta has put on a few pounds in retirement. He attended a few East Sycamore games at first, but felt he was too much of a distraction. He does enjoy getting to watch some of his former players on television, though. He and his wife have traveled many places in the last ten years, including the Grand

Canyon, Cancun, and Alaska. This summer they're going to New Zealand and renting a camper van. His wife particularly wants to see the hobbit village from that Lord of the Rings movie.

Martha Sullivan did not receive a scholarship offer from Georgia Tech, for which she is thankful. While Colorado State never made the NCAA tournament while she was there, and Martha never put up the same big numbers she did at West Sycamore, she considers her time at Colorado State to be the best years of her life. She is now married, living in Boulder, Colorado, and working as a computer programmer for Oracle.

Chamique Lennox played three more years at East Sycamore, and was named captain her senior year. She earned a scholarship to Santa Clara University, where she started her final two years. She tried out unsuccessfully for FC Kansas City in the National Women's Soccer League (NWSL), and is currently living in Oakland, California, teaching 4th grade. She and her girlfriend are thinking about buying a house.

Susan Douglas lived with the Galtons during her senior year at West Sycamore. She helped the team win State, and received a scholarship to the University of Portland. UP reached the NCAA tournament all four years she was there, losing in the championship game her senior year. Susan spent one year as a bench player for the Portland Thorns in the NWSL before retiring to become a massage therapist. She and her husband still live in Portland, in a little house with a garden out back. They take in foster kids.

Estefania Higuain played one more year at East Sycamore, earning a scholarship to Florida State University, where she was a two-year starter. She spent two years as a bench player for Seattle in the NWSL, then left soccer to attend dental school. She's currently working as an orthodontist in Olympia, Washington, where she plays soccer twice a week in a women's rec league. She's the best player on her team.

Destinee Jones was a three-year starter at the University of Maryland, then spent three years as an occasional starter for Boston in the NWSL before a ruptured Achilles convinced her to retire. She's currently living in Greenbelt, Maryland, and working for the non-profit organization Mercy Corps. She still loves pumpkin spice lattes.

Kaitlyn Baker was a four-year starter at the University of Oklahoma, and captain her final two years. Currently, she's the starting central midfielder and captain for Chicago in the NWSL. They lost in the championship game last year, but she says they're winning the title this year. "You can print that, actually. *Baker Guarantees Title.* I welcome the pressure."

Clementine Thiamale was named captain her senior year at West Sycamore, and received a scholarship to the University of Minnesota, where she was a three-year starter. She played two years for Orlando in the NWSL before moving to France, where she's an occasional starter for the Paris Saint-Germain women's team. She also has 62 caps for the Cote d'Ivoire national team, which is currently ranked 40th in the world, and qualified for the most recent World Cup. She recently started dating a French man named Karim, who she likes quite a bit.

Lisa Roney was named captain her senior year at East Sycamore, and received a scholarship to the University of Southern California, where she started all four years and was named an All-American twice. Currently, she plays professionally for Boston in the NWSL, has 47 caps for the US Women's National Team (USWNT), and was a bench player at the last two World Cups.

Catalina Forero was a four-year starter and three-time All-American at Stanford University. In both her sophomore and junior seasons, Stanford was knocked out of the NCAA tournament by UNC and their star goalkeeper, Hayley Swanson, but in her senior season, the team finally broke through and became NCAA champions, beating Hayley and UNC in the final. Professionally, Catalina played two years for Houston in the NWSL before moving to England, where she currently plays for Arsenal in the English women's league. She has 104 caps with the USWNT and was the starting center back in the last two Women's World Cups. One-time World Cup champion.

Maria Solana played one more year at West Sycamore, winning both the state title and her second straight Player of the Year award. Soon after, she moved to Spain to join the FC Barcelona women's team, where she's been starting for the last eight years. The team has won the Superliga Feminina five of those eight years, and Maria has won FIFA World Player of the Year twice. She has 95 caps for the Colombian national team, which is currently ranked third in the world and made the semifinals of the last Women's World Cup, where they lost to the US. In an interview with *Sports Illustrated*, Maria said, "Before West Sycamore, I was just a nobody girl from a tiny village in Colombia. After West Sycamore, I was Maria Solana."

C.I. DeMann

Connect with the author online

I'm all over the place online. Search me out on Twitter, Facebook, YouTube, and Goodreads.

I've also got a soccer column called "Six Degrees" at stumptownfooty.com and a radio show called "Six Degrees of Rockination" at kpsu.org.

And if you're looking to buy another book – my novel *A Punk Rock Love Song*, perhaps? – you can use powells.com, Amazon, Smashwords, Apple, Barnes & Noble, Kobo, and assorted others.

C.I. DeMann